Dear *Skinnybones* fans,

Can you believe it? This year marks the *fifteenth* anniversary of *Skinnybones*! It seems as if just last week I was typing away (on a broken-down portable typewriter), trying to pound out enough jokes to keep Alex Frankovitch rolling for twelve chapters.

I was a brand-new author back then, so you can imagine my surprise when the book was published and the fan mail started pouring in. You wouldn't believe how many readers wrote hilarious tales of falling on the floor laughing as they read about Alex's crazy stunts. I loved it!

But over the years, I began to notice a slight shift in some of my *Skinnybones* mail. Mixed in with the usual funny comments came questions like this one:

> *Dear Barbara Park,*
> *I loved reading SKINNYBONES...but who is Steve Garvey? I've never heard of him. Is he a real ballplayer, or did you just make him up?*

And this one:

> *Dear Barbara Park,*
> *Our class has a question about SKINNYBONES. In Chapter 3...what are wax lips? Are they some kind of disguise or something?*

Oh, no! I thought. *Has Alex been around so long that his humor is becoming... outdated?* It was a chilling idea. And afterward every time I looked at my copy of *Skinnybones*, I could almost hear Alex shouting, "WELL, DON'T JUST SIT THERE! DO SOMETHING!!!"

So finally I did. I spent last summer revisiting my smart-alecky friend and "freshening up" his act a bit. I wrote him some new jokes, polished up a few paragraphs, and tweaked bits and pieces of dialogue along the way. I hadn't had that much fun since I created the original story!

So Happy anniversary, Alex Frankovitch! You're no longer caught in a time warp.

And to *Skinnybones* fans everywhere...thanks for fifteen years of laughing along! You're the best!

Barbara Park

Kids love Barbara Park's books so much, they've given them all these awards:

Arizona Young Reader's Award

Georgia Children's Book Award

Great Stone Face Award (New Hampshire)

IRA-CBC Children's Choice

IRA Young Adults' Choice

Maud Hart Lovelace Award (Minnesota)

Milner Award (Georgia)

Nevada Children's Book Award

OMAR Award (Indiana)

Rhode Island Children's Book Award

Tennessee Children's Choice Book Award

Texas Bluebonnet Award

Utah Children's Book Award

Young Hoosier Book Award (Indiana)

Skinnybones

Barbara Park

Random House
New York

A RANDOM HOUSE BOOK

visit us on the web! www.randomhouse.com/kids

Educators and librarians, for a variety of teaching tools, visit us at
www.randomhouse.com/teachers

Library of Congress Catalog Card Number: 97-065624
ISBN: 0-375-80672-5
RL: 4.3

Printed in the United States of America
May 2000
10 9 8 7 6 5 4 3 2 1
OPM

To Steven and David, for all your inspiration

chapter one

ME AND THE KID WITH THE WOODEN NOSE

MY CAT EATS KITTY FRITTERS BECAUSE...

If she didn't eat Kitty Fritters, she would die of star-vation.

Kitty Fritters is the only cat food my mother will buy. She buys it because she says it's cheap. She says she doesn't care how it tastes, or what it's made out of. My mother is not the kind of person who believes that an animal is a member of the family. She is one of those people who thinks a cat is just a cat.

I have an aunt who thinks that her cat is a real person. Every time we go over there, she has the cat dressed up in this little sweater that says PRINCESS KITTY on the front.

This aunt of mine wouldn't be caught dead giv-

ing her cat Kitty Fritters. She says that Kitty Fritters taste like rubber. I'd hate to think that my aunt has actually tasted Kitty Fritters herself, but how else would she know? My mother says that my aunt has a screw loose somewhere.

Anyway, I think you should keep on making Kitty Fritters as long as there are people like my mother, who don't think cats mind eating rubber.

THE END

After I finished writing my comments, I went to the closet and took the bag of Kitty Fritters off the bottom shelf. I turned to the back of the bag and read the rest of the directions. It said:

COMPLETE THIS SENTENCE:
MY CAT EATS KITTY FRITTERS BECAUSE...
Then print your name and address on the entry
blank enclosed in this bag. Mail your entry to:

KITTY FRITTERS TV CONTEST
P.O. Box 2343
Philadelphia, Pennsylvania 19103

I dug down into the bag, trying to find the entry blank, but I couldn't feel it anywhere. I tried again, reaching into the other side this time. But still no luck.

Finally, I got so frustrated, I dumped the entire twenty-five-pound bag of cat food out onto the kitchen floor. Even then, I must have sifted through about a million fritters before I found the stupid thing.

At last, I put it on the table and began to fill it out.

NAME: Alex Frankovitch
ADDRESS: 2567 Delaney Street
CITY: Phoenix STATE: Arizona ZIP: 85000

Just as I finished up, I heard the cat scratching at the door. I figured she had probably smelled the odor of fritters all the way down the block.

"Go away, Fluffy!" I shouted. "You can't eat right now. I'm busy!"

I had to get the cat food mess cleaned up before my mother got home.

"Alex Frankovitch! You open this door!" shouted Fluffy.

Fluffy? Fluffy was *talking* now?

No...wait! It was my *mother!*

I hurried to let her in.

"Why were you scratching?" I asked as she hurried past me.

It was a stupid question. She was carrying two bags of groceries.

"I wasn't *scratching,* Alex," she answered. "I was trying to open the door with my foot."

After putting the groceries on the counter, my mother spotted the millions of little fritters scattered all over the floor. All things considered, I think she took it pretty well.

"Been fixing yourself a little snack?" she asked dryly.

I had to think fast. Basically, there were two ways of handling this situation. First, I could try to get her to laugh the whole thing off. If that failed, I would move on to Plan B: Blame It on Fluffy.

"Snack? What snack?" I asked. "I haven't been fixing a snack."

"I mean all those Kitty Fritters, Alex," she snapped. "I mean that huge mess all over the floor."

I looked around. "Floor? What floor?" I asked.

This was where the laughing was supposed to start. Unfortunately, it didn't.

Mom glared.

"I'm waiting," she said.

On to Plan B…

"Oh…*those* Kitty Fritters!" I said, pointing. "Well, you're not going to believe this, Mom, but I was in the other room watching TV, when all of a sudden I heard this loud crash in the kitchen. I ran in here just in time to see Fluffy sprinting out the back door. That's when I looked down and saw this giant mess of fritters all over the floor."

My mother crossed her arms. She didn't say anything for a minute.

"Are you *sure* that's what happened, Alex?" she asked, finally. "Are you positive?"

Oh, man! I couldn't believe this! She was actually going to *buy* it! My mother was going to buy this whole insane story! For the very first time, I was going to get away with something! Usually I never get away with anything!

"Positive, Mom. Honest. That's exactly what happened. The cat must have tried to eat out of the bag and she knocked the whole thing over."

Slowly—*very* slowly—Mom walked over and put her arm around my shoulder. "In that case, would you mind doing me a little favor?" she asked.

I started backing away.

"Oh, no. Come on, Mom. You're not going to make me clean this mess up, are you? That's not fair. I already told you I didn't do it."

"No, Alex. That's not the favor," she said. "What I would like you to do is to go get Fluffy out of the car and bring her inside. I took her to the vet to get some shots, and she's still a little groggy."

Then my mother just stood there and grinned.

Not a nice grin, though. One of those "Ha! Caught-you-in-a-big-fat-lie" kind of grins.

Now, most people would probably give up at this point. But not me. No way. A liar at my skill level never gives up without a struggle.

My mouth dropped all the way open and I managed an actual gasp.

"Are you kidding, Mother? Fluffy? Fluffy is in the car?" I said. "Man, I cannot believe this!"

Mom narrowed her eyes. "Can't believe what, Alex? Can't believe that you've been caught in another ridiculous lie?"

I gasped again.

"Lie? What lie? What are you talking about, Mom?" I asked indignantly. "No. The thing I can't believe is that one of Fluffy's little friends would come in here, make a big mess, and then try to run away and blame it on the Fluffster! I'm telling you, when I find out which neighborhood cat did this, he is really going to pay."

I hurried outside and got Fluffy from the car. As I walked back into the house, I kept talking to the cat so that my mother wouldn't have a chance to say anything.

"Fluffy, you're not going to believe this, but one of your little kitty pals almost got you in very big trouble. If you ask me, I think it was Mr. Fuzzy, from down the street. I've always thought that Mr. Fuzzy was the shifty type."

"Alex?" said my mother.

"Yes?"

"Give up."

"Give up? What do you mean, give up?"

"I mean, you're making a complete fool of yourself," she said. "I mean I'm actually embarrassed for you."

I paused for a minute. "So what are you saying? Are you saying you don't believe me?"

"Let me put it this way," answered my mother. "If you were Pinocchio, right now we could saw off your nose and have enough firewood to last the winter."

With that, she handed me a broom and started out of the room.

"By the way, if it will make you feel any better, I enjoyed the part about Mr. Fuzzy," she said over her shoulder.

I thought about it.

It didn't make me feel better.

As soon as she was gone, I started sweeping the Kitty Fritters back into the bag. Meanwhile, Fluffy had begun to eat every single fritter in sight. I'm not kidding. No matter how fast I swept, I just couldn't get the food into the bag fast enough. Fluffy was sucking them up like she was a Dustbuster or something.

It took about ten minutes before I was totally finished cleaning up the floor. But Fluffy never stopped eating…not until the very last Kitty Fritter was out of sight.

Just as I was putting the bag back, my mother came in to inspect the floor.

Fluffy made a weird noise.

My mother frowned. "What's wrong with her?"

I shrugged. "I don't know. It's probably all those Kitty Fritters she ate while I was trying to get them cleaned up."

Mom's eyes widened. "Oh, Alex, no! Those things will swell up in her stomach and make her sick! She's not supposed to have too many!"

She looked seriously worried.

I would have been seriously worried too. But just then Fluffy walked over to where I was standing, and she threw up on my shoe.

It was the most disgusting thing that ever happened to me.

My mother busted out laughing.

"Not funny!" I yelled.

But Mom couldn't help herself. She left the room all doubled over. I'm not kidding. For a mother, she can act extremely immature at times.

Anyway, as it turned out, she was laughing so hard, she forgot to punish me for lying.

I knew getting her to laugh would work

It's just too bad I couldn't have done it without getting hurled on.

chapter two
SHOWIN' AND TELLIN'

The first time I ever remember making people laugh was in kindergarten. Each morning, the teacher would ask if anyone had anything special for Show and Tell.

At first I was pretty shy about it. I would just sit there quietly at my desk and keep my mouth shut. But there were lots of kids who didn't.

Like there was this one kid who we called Weird Peter Donnelly. Every single day, when the teacher asked if anyone had anything for Show and Tell, Weird Peter Donnelly would raise his hand.

Mostly, he brought in his hobbies. Weird Peter had the stupidest hobbies in the whole world. One of them was collecting different-colored sweater fuzz. Scary, right?

One day he brought his fuzz collection to school. He kept it in a shoe box. When he passed it around, I felt stupid just looking at it.

Then all of a sudden, I got this funny idea. Just as I was about to pass the box to the next person, I pretended that I was going to sneeze.

"AH…AH…AH…AHCHOO!"

I sneezed right smack in the middle of Weird Peter Donnelly's sweater fuzz! Fuzz balls went flying everywhere!

The whole class went nuts laughing.

Weird Peter freaked out. He ran over to my desk and began gathering up fuzz and putting it back in his box.

The teacher told me to help him, but I was laughing too hard to get out of my chair. I had to admit, making people laugh was a lot more fun than sitting quietly at my desk.

From then on, I began to use Show and Tell to tell the class funny things that had happened to me. When I ran out of true things to tell, I started making them up.

One time I told the class that my father was Mr. Potato Head. I don't know what made me say such a stupid thing. It just came out.

The teacher made me sit down. She said that there was a big difference between Show and Tell and Show and Blatantly-Lie-Right-to-Our-Faces.

Personally, I don't think teachers like it when their students are funnier than they are. So far I've been funnier than every teacher I've ever had, and not one of them has liked me. My goal in life is to try and find a teacher who appreciates my sense of humor.

Last year—in fifth grade—I had a teacher named Miss Henderson. Out of all the teachers I've ever had, Miss Henderson is the one who disliked me the most.

It makes sense, though. In fifth grade, I was the funniest I've ever been.

On the very first day of school, I knew we weren't going to get along. Miss Henderson made everyone stand up next to their desk and introduce themselves to the class. You had to say your name, where you were born, and something about your family. How lame is that?

Allison Martin went first. She said, "My name is Allison Martin. I was born right here in Phoenix, and I have two brothers."

Oooh...let me write that down, I thought to myself.

Then Brenda Ferguson stood up. "My name is Brenda Ferguson. I was born in California, and I have a baby sister."

And blah, blah, blah, I thought.

This had to be the most boring first day of school I'd ever had. After about six kids had spoken, I just couldn't stand it anymore. I raised my hand.

"Yes?" asked Miss Henderson. "You there, in the yellow shirt."

I looked down at my shirt. Yup. That was me, all right.

"Miss Henderson? I was just thinking...maybe we should try to tell something a little more interesting about ourselves, instead of just the usual stuff," I said.

Miss Henderson considered it a second. Then she gave me a little smile.

"Okay," she said, "why don't you start us off? Tell us who you are and something interesting about yourself."

Wow! I thought. *Maybe for once, I've got a teacher who is actually going to appreciate me.*

"Okay. I'm Alex Frankovitch," I said. "I brought a sandwich for lunch today. And I'd just like everyone to know that my bologna has a first name...it's O-s-c-a-r."

The whole class cracked up at once. Miss Henderson had to beat on her desk with a ruler to quiet everyone down. I almost felt sorry for her.

That was before she came over to my desk, bent

13

down next to my ear, and whispered, "I've got your number, funny boy."

As soon as she got the class under control, we started all over with the same boring stuff we had been doing before.

After about an hour, we were almost finished. That's when I first saw T.J. Stoner. He was sitting all the way in the back of the room, so he was the last person to talk about himself.

He stood up real slow and cool. "My name is T.J. Stoner," he said. "I just moved here from San Diego, and I have an older brother who plays baseball for the Atlanta Braves."

Then he sat back down just as slow and cool as when he'd stood up.

I knew right away I wasn't going to like old T.J. Stoner.

Miss Henderson did, though. She was totally impressed.

"Really, T.J.?" she gushed. "Why don't you tell us a little bit more about him?"

T.J. stood up again. "Well, his name's Matt Stoner and this is his second year in the majors. He's a pinch-hitter," he added.

"How exciting!" said Miss Henderson. "Do you play baseball, too, T.J.?"

He nodded. "I'm a pitcher. Last year my team

won the California State Championship, and I was voted the Most Valuable Player."

By this time I was ready to barf.

I raised my hand again and waved it all over the place.

You could tell that Miss Henderson didn't want to call on me, but I was pretty hard to ignore.

"Okay, Alex. What?" she asked, annoyed.

"Well, I just thought that the class might like to know that I play baseball, too," I said.

Miss Henderson stared. "So?"

"So last season, I played right field," I told her. "I didn't get voted MVP. But I *did* come in second in the swimsuit competition."

That did it. The whole class went crazy again. Brenda Ferguson laughed so hard she fell off her chair.

Two people didn't laugh at all, though.

One was T.J. Stoner.

The other one was Miss Henderson.

I sat down and shut up.

I may be funny. But I'm not totally stupid.

chapter three

REEKIN' AND STINKIN' AND A LITTLE DO-SI-DO

Sometimes I think it would be fun to be a school principal. Especially in the summer. In the summer, a school principal spends his time composing lists of all the kids in the school who hate each other. Then he makes sure they end up in the same class together.

My principal really must have had a good laugh when he put T.J. and me together again this year. Ever since my music teacher sent me to the office for getting my head caught in a tuba, my principal hasn't seemed to like me much.

When I first discovered the news that T.J. was in my class, I went straight to my mother. I was hoping that she would call the school and have me switched.

But no such luck. All Mom did was tell me I

should try to *ignore* him. Seriously. She's always giving me great advice like that. Then she hands me my lunch, shoves me out the door, and her problems are over for the day. *Mine* are just beginning.

Last year, T.J. Stoner grew to be the biggest kid in the whole fifth grade. When I began to notice how gigantic he was getting, I decided it might not be a bad idea to try to get on his good side. But T.J. didn't seem too interested. When I asked if he wanted to be friends, I believe his exact words were, "Get out of my face, toad-sucker."

"Would that be a *no?*" I asked.

T.J. grabbed me by the shoulders.

"That would be an *I hate your slimy guts, Frankovitch,*" he said.

I smiled. "Oh, come on, T.J. Can't our slimy guts be friends?" I asked.

T.J. didn't think that was quite as funny as I did. I could tell by the way he pushed me down and pinned my face under his foot.

"You think you're such a funny guy, don't you, you skinny little bag of bones?" he said.

It's too bad my mother wasn't there. Maybe she could have told me how to ignore someone's Nike in your mouth.

I think the worst thing about being in the same room

with T.J. is having him in my P.E. class. I hate to admit it, but he really *is* a great athlete. For a kid, T.J. Stoner is the best ballplayer I've ever seen.

There's only one sport that I'm better at than T.J. It's square dancing.

I figure I can count square dancing as a sport because we do it in P.E. You ought to see me. I can do-si-do better than any other kid in the whole school.

One time I asked the P.E. teacher, Mr. McGuinsky, if he had ever thought about starting a school square dancing team. I told him that if he did, I would volunteer to be the team captain.

Mr. McGuinsky thought I was being a smart aleck. He told me to sit my butt down and shut up. In case you never noticed, P.E. teachers enjoy saying "butt" a lot.

Anyway, I do play other sports besides square dancing. Like T.J., I've played Little League baseball for six years now. But to tell you the truth, I'm not exactly what you'd call a real good athlete. Actually, I'm not even real okay. Basically, what I'm trying to say here is, I stink.

I've got proof, too. Every single year that I've played Little League, I've received the trophy for Most Improved Player.

Now, at first, you might think that means I sound

pretty good…which is what *I* used to think, too. But over the past six years, I've noticed that none of the really *outstanding* players ever gets the Most Improved Player award. And the reason is simple. The outstanding players are already so outstanding they can't *improve* much. Let's face it, the only players on a team who can improve are the ones who reek to begin with.

Last year, at the end of baseball season, I tried to explain how I felt to my father. We were sitting together at the Little League awards ceremony, and the announcer was calling the names of all the players who were going to be receiving trophies.

I started squirming around in my seat.

"Just relax, Alex," said my dad. "It won't be the end of the world if you don't win Most Improved again this year."

He didn't get it at all.

"No, see, that's just it, Dad," I said, trying to explain. "I don't *want* to get Most Improved again. I mean, I don't want to sound like a poor sport or anything, but if they call my name, let's just pretend we're not here. What do you say, Dad? We could do that, couldn't we?"

I could tell by his face that he was shocked.

"Pretend we're not here?" he blustered. "Why in the world would we pretend we're not here?"

"Shh…Dad…not so loud! It's just embarrassing to get another Improved award, that's all. I don't want it."

"You don't want it? What do you mean, you don't want it? I can't believe I'm hearing this. How ungrateful can you get, Alex? Do you know how many kids here would love to get that award tonight?"

"Yeah, Dad. I know," I answered. "But that's only because nobody else has ever gotten it five times in a row. Don't you see a pattern here? Every year I start out totally *reeking* and end up only *stinking*. Then the next year I start out reeking again. Is that supposed to make me proud?"

All of a sudden, we heard it.

My name…being called over the microphone!

"ALEX FRANKOVITCH. MOST IMPROVED PLAYER AWARD FOR TEAM NUMBER SEVEN—PRESTON'S PEST CONTROL!"

Quick as anything, I slid down in my seat so that no one could see me. My father grabbed my arm to make me stand up. But I doubled over and put my head between my knees.

"ALEX FRANKOVITCH? IS ALEX HERE?" the announcer called again.

My father jumped up from his seat and pointed at me. At least that's what I *think* he did. By then,

I was wadded into a tight little ball.

"HERE HE IS, RIGHT HERE! ALEX FRANKOVITCH IS RIGHT HERE!" my dad yelled.

Everyone started clapping. A few of the kids who knew me started shouting, "WE WANT ALEX…WE WANT ALEX!"

Finally, I just had no choice. I stood up and started making my way down the bleachers. On my way down, I decided that me and dear old Dad were *finished*. Kaput! Finito!

When I got to the bottom, I spotted T.J. Stoner. He had already received his zillionth Most Valuable Player trophy and was sitting in the front row, pointing at me and laughing. Just pointing and laughing.

I hated it. I mean, I just couldn't let him get away with making fun of me like that, you know? So I decided the only thing to do was pretend that I was actually enjoying myself.

I walked to the middle of the gym floor, turned around, and started taking bows and throwing kisses. Then I walked over to the table to pick up my trophy.

The announcer handed me the microphone. I was supposed to say thank you. But instead, I took the microphone…

Held it up to my mouth…

And burped.

The whole audience went nuts like you wouldn't believe. At least that's the way it sounded. But looking back, it was probably only the kids who went nuts. Grownups don't usually think burping is all that comical.

Anyway, after I threw a few more kisses, I ducked out the gym door and walked home.

I knew I was in big trouble. So I went straight to my room and waited for my father. I just wanted to get it over with.

While I was waiting, I made a sign and hung it on the outside of my door. The sign read:

THIS ROOM BELONGS TO ALEX FRANKOVITCH
THE ONLY BOY IN THE WHOLE WORLD
WHO HAS GONE FROM
TOTALLY REEKING TO ONLY STINKING
<u>6</u> YEARS IN A ROW.

When Dad saw the sign, he didn't bother coming into my room to yell at me. I guess he figured I already felt bad enough.

For once, he figured right.

chapter four
THEY'RE MAGICALLY DELICIOUS

For me, the worst part about belonging to Little League is the uniforms. Every year at the first practice, the same thing happens. The coach shouts out your name, and you have to yell out what size you wear. Right in front of *everyone,* I mean. You have to yell either large...medium...or small.

This year there were a total of twelve kids on my team. And the way it looked to me, there would probably be two larges, nine mediums, and one eensy-weensy, itsy-bitsy, practically-the-size-a-baby-would-wear. (Me.)

Every single year, I am always the smallest kid on the team. I mean it. For the first five years of my life, I thought I was a leprechaun.

I remember when I was in kindergarten, our

teacher asked us to cut out magazine pictures of what we thought we would be when we grew up.

Most of the boys in my class brought in pictures of baseball or football players. A few others brought in pictures of policemen.

I brought in a picture of the Lucky Charms guy. I cut it off the front of the cereal box.

My teacher was pretty worried about it, too. She called me right up to her desk.

"Alex, what is this a picture of?" she asked.

"It's the Lucky Charms guy," I said.

She closed her eyes. "That's what I was afraid of."

"Oh, you don't have to be afraid of the Lucky Charms guy, Mrs. Hurley," I said. "He gets on your nerves, but he's not really dangerous."

Mrs. Hurley shook her head. "No, Alex. What I don't understand is why you *want* to be a leprechaun."

"I don't. I want to be a pilot," I told her.

"Then why did you bring this picture?" asked Mrs. Hurley.

"Because that's what I'm *going* to be," I explained. "That's what you told us to do, right? You said to bring in a picture of what we were *going* to be when we grow up."

Mrs. Hurley called my mother.

As soon as I walked in the door that afternoon, Mom sat me right down and we had a talk about being small.

"Alex, I know that you think you're too short. But that's only because you haven't started to grow as much as some of the other kids yet. Everyone grows at different speeds. But, believe me, you *are* going to grow. I promise."

She took me by the hand and led me to the kitchen. Then she stood me up against the wall near the corner and told me not to move.

At first, I thought this was some weird new punishment she'd read about in one of those parenting magazines. But instead, she got a pencil and made a mark on the wall at the very top of my head. When I moved away, she wrote the date beside it.

"Okay," she said. "Just to prove to you that you're growing, we're going to measure you every six months. That way you will be able to see the change for yourself."

Well, all I can say is, six months is a long time to wait. Especially when you're worried about having to go flitting around the countryside dancing a jig in a green top hat.

When the day finally came to measure me again, I was nervous as anything.

My mother stood me up against the wall in the

25

same spot where I had been measured before. Then she carefully made another pencil mark.

I turned to look.

Half an inch! I had grown almost a whole half an inch!

I started jumping around all over the place.

Mom looked as relieved as me. "*Now* do you believe me?" she asked. "Does this prove to you that you're getting taller?"

"Yeah!" I said. "Now all I have to do is gain some weight and grow big feet, and I'll practically be a real boy."

My mother threw up her hands in frustration. "I give up, Alex! I swear! You're never satisfied!"

Sometimes she just doesn't understand me at all. Being small is *not* an easy thing to be. Especially when you're in Little League, and you have to shout out your size in front of your whole entire team.

"Alex Frankovitch?" called my coach. "Small, medium, or large?"

No. I couldn't. I just couldn't shout *small* again. Not in *sixth* grade.

I swallowed hard. Then I made my voice as deep as I could and yelled, "Large!"

The coach looked up and gave me the eyeball. "Excuse me, son…but did you say 'large'?"

"Yes, sir. Large. That's what I said. Alex

Frankovitch takes a large," I repeated.

"Are you sure, Mr. Frankovitch? Are you absolutely, positively sure that *large* is the size you usually order?" he persisted.

"Yup. Yup, I am. I'm absolutely, positively sure. Large. That's the size I order. I order a large. Alex Frankovitch orders a large."

The coach rolled his eyes and shook his head. I'm pretty sure I heard him mutter the word *bean-brain* too. But I really didn't care what he thought. The important thing was that, finally—after all these years—I hadn't had to shout out the word *small*.

I couldn't wait for the day the uniforms came in. I was sure it would be the best day of my life. I even had a dream about it.

In my dream, the coach had all the uniforms arranged in just two piles—smalls and larges—and he was calling out names and sizes. As soon as you heard your name, you had to go to the correct pile and pick up your uniform.

"ALEX FRANKOVITCH! LARGE!" he announced, loud as anything.

I stood up real slow and cool. Then I strolled over to the large pile to choose my pants and shirt. But when I got there, I found out that mine was the only uniform in the large pile. The *only one*, get it?

All the other guys were smalls! And here's where it gets good...because when I reached out to pick up my large shirt, the whole team jumped up and started cheering! Because of how *large* I was and all!

It was the best dream I ever had. I swear. And, when the team uniforms finally came in—after three whole weeks of waiting—at least part of my dream was about to come true. I'd have my large shirt!

I was the first kid at practice that day. When I arrived, my coach was already arranging everything in piles. My heart started pounding like crazy. It was just like in my dream! I felt as if I had seen into the future or something.

As soon as he was finished, the coach told us to line up single-file. Then one by one, we were to go to the correct pile and pick out a uniform. I have to admit, this wasn't quite as good as if he had announced my name and size. But still, all I really cared about was getting my *large*.

As soon as it was my turn, I rushed right over and grabbed a large shirt and pair of pants. Then I sort of hung around the large pile for a while just so everyone would notice.

Finally, when all the piles were gone, the coach told us to check our uniforms to make sure we had gotten the right size.

That's when I heard some of the guys starting to laugh. When I turned around, I saw Randy Tubbs trying to pull his new shirt over his head. It was stuck on his ears, and his eyes were bulging out where it was cutting off his circulation.

The coach helped Randy pull the shirt off. He looked inside to see what size it was.

"This is a small, Randy," he said. "You're supposed to have a large."

Randy shrugged. "It's all that was left," he said.

Right away, the coach started looking on his list, trying to figure out what had happened. This wasn't good. This wasn't good at all.

Slowly, I started backing off the field. But the coach spotted me.

"Hold it, Alex! Wait!" he called. "Would you bring your uniform back here a minute, please?"

I felt sick. Sicker than I'd ever felt before. But there was nothing I could do except go back.

Reluctantly, I handed him my shirt and pants and pointed at the tag. "See, Coach? See? It's a large, just like you ordered for me," I said.

The coach just shook his head. "Alex, I ordered you a small. A large would eat you up and spit you out."

Then he gave my uniform to Randy and handed

me the eensy-weensy, itsy-bitsy, practically-the-size-a-baby-would-wear…small.

It was one of the lowest moments of my life.

When I got home, I went to my room and tried it on. Thanks to Randy and his giant dome, the neck was all stretched out, and it drooped down to my stomach.

My mother came in and told me not to worry. She said the shirt would probably shrink when it was washed.

As soon as she left, my pants fell down.

chapter five

HAS ANYONE SEEN MY VELVET PILLOW?

T.J. Stoner brags about his baseball team more than any kid I've ever known in my whole life. So what if his team hasn't lost a game all year? It doesn't mean they won just because of *him*. Everybody knows that just one person can't make the difference between a winning team and a losing team. After all, every single team I've ever been on has come in last place. And I don't care what anyone says, all those teams didn't lose just because of *me*...probably.

Anyway, this year I know for a fact that I am not the worst player on my team. The worst player on my team is Ryan Brady. Ryan broke his arm the first game of the season, and now all he does is sit on the bench. I'm sure I help the team out more than Ryan does...probably.

I play right field. A lot of kids automatically think that if you play in the outfield, it means you can't catch or throw. But my father says that's ridiculous. He says that outfielders are just as good as infielders. He told me that when he was a boy, he played in right field just like me.

That really doesn't make me feel much better, though. I've seen Dad play. He can't catch or throw.

My mother says that when people like T.J. Stoner brag, they're just trying to get attention. As usual, she says to ignore them. But for some reason, whenever I hear T.J. start to brag about his baseball team, I just can't seem to keep my big mouth shut.

Like one day, a few weeks ago, I heard him spouting off to a bunch of kids at the playground.

"My coach told me I'm one of the best Little League pitchers in the whole country this year," he bragged.

As soon as I heard him say it, my mouth went right out of control. I started talking real loud to my friend Brian Dunlop.

"HEY, BRIAN. I FORGOT TO TELL YOU ABOUT MY BASEBALL PRACTICE LAST NIGHT. MY COACH LET ME TRY OUT FOR PITCHER AND HE SAID I HAD ONE OF THE BEST CURVE BALLS HE'S EVER SEEN."

Okay, *I know* it was a dumb thing to say. But

Brian wasn't much help. He fell right on the ground and started laughing himself sick.

"You?" he roared. "You…you…you…*pitched?*"

T.J. came strolling over with this big, smirky grin on his face. He bent down and tapped Brian on the head. "'Scuse me. But did I hear Skinnybones say that he can throw a curve ball?" he asked.

Brian held his stomach and busted out laughing all over again.

T.J.'s smirk got bigger. "Hey, Frankovitch. How'd you like to make a little deal?" he said.

I shook my head and started to walk away. "Nope. Sorry, T.J. No deals. I'm gonna have to tell you what I've been telling everybody else today. No matter how hard you beg, I cannot pitch for your team. My coach made me sign a contract."

Brian let out another wild hoot of laughter. Apparently, the idea of me pitching was a lot more amusing than I thought.

It's not like I've never tried it before. Just last week, I practiced pitching with my dad. It didn't actually work out that good, though. Most of the balls I threw didn't make it to the plate. The one that did, beaned my father on the head.

"What kind of stupid pitch do you call that?" Dad yelled.

"That would be my bean ball!" I yelled back.

33

We packed up our stuff right then and went home. I'm not kidding. The man cannot take a joke.

Anyway, T.J. kept on bugging me and bugging me. "Come on, Alex," he pleaded. "Just listen to my deal. What have you got to lose?"

By this time a bunch of kids had started to gather.

"Okay. Fine. Tell me your deal, T.J. But make it snappy. It's almost time for Brian to massage my pitching arm."

Brian went off in another fit of hysterics.

"All right. Here it is," said T.J. "Since both of us are such good pitchers, why don't we have a contest after school to see who's the best? We'll even get a couple of kids to be the official umpires. What do you say, Alex? That'll be fun, don't you think?"

Oh, geez, what a mess! If I said no, everyone would know I was a liar. But if I said yes, everyone would be able to see how weak I threw. Somehow I had to get out of this.

I hit myself in the head. "Oh, man. I just remembered. My coach told me not to tire my arm out by being in any stupid pitching contests. I'm mostly just supposed to rest it on a velvet pillow. Thank you anyway, though. See ya."

I started to walk away, but T.J. grabbed me by the shoulders.

"I'm not *asking* you, Frankovitch. I'm *telling* you. You get one of your friends, and I'll get one of mine. They'll be the umps. I'll meet you at the Little League field after school. If you don't show, we'll all know it's because you're a liar and you can't throw a curve."

As he turned to leave, he stopped and looked back at me. "*Be* there, chump."

After everyone left, I looked down at Brian. He was still on the ground.

I reached out my hand to help him up.

"Thank you, Brian. You were very supportive," I said dryly.

Brian nodded his head "you're welcome." His sides were still hurting from all that laughing.

"Geez, Brian. If you think this is funny, wait until you see my curve ball," I said.

This time both of us started laughing.

I figured I'd better laugh now while I still had the chance.

chapter six

ALL WOUND UP AND
NOWHERE TO THROW

I kept praying that school would last forever that day. But before I knew it, the three o'clock bell rang, and my teacher dismissed the class.

I stayed at my desk until everyone was gone. I just *had* to think of some reason to stay after school. I *had* to get out of that pitching contest.

"Mrs. Grayson, how would you like some help cleaning the boards and erasers this afternoon?" I asked hopefully.

"No thanks, Alex. I've got a meeting to go to," she replied.

I tried to act shocked. "Mrs. Grayson, I'm surprised at you!" I said. "You don't mean you're going off and leaving this room in this condition, do you? The place looks like a pig sty."

Mrs. Grayson closed her eyes. "Please, Alex. Don't start, okay? I'm really in a hurry."

She tried to usher me out the door, but I kept dragging my feet.

"Yes…well…um…exactly what kind of meeting are you going to, Mrs. Grayson?" I asked. "Maybe I could tag along."

"It's a teachers' meeting, Alex. And you can't tag along. No students allowed. Now move it. Please. I don't want to be late."

Suddenly, my face brightened. "Wait a second, Mrs. G. I'm getting an idea here. Maybe you could sneak me into the meeting. That would be kinda fun, don't you think? That way, if things get boring, you and I could play tic-tac-toe in the back of the room."

Mrs. Grayson narrowed her eyes suspiciously. "Alex? Is there some *reason* that you don't want to leave school today? Are you in some sort of trouble?"

"Trouble? Me? Oh, no, Mrs. Grayson. Not me. No trouble here. Nope. None at all. Zero trouble. Honest. I was just trying to make your meeting a little more fun, that's all."

"Well, thank you anyway," she said. "But I'll be fine. Really."

Reluctantly, I stood up. "All righty, then," I said. "I guess I'll just let you be on your way. That is, unless you'd like me to wait until your meeting's over so I can help you with the boards…which I wouldn't mind doing at all, Mrs. Grayson. 'Cause that's the kind of guy I am. Like right this minute, if you were to say, 'Sit down and wait till my meeting's over,' that's exactly what I would do, Mrs. G. I would sit down right here and I would…"

Mrs. Grayson put her hands over her ears. "GO HOME, ALEX!" she blurted out.

So that was pretty much that.

I went home and got my ball and glove.

Then I called Brian and told him to meet me at the Little League field. It made me sick to have to go through with this, but there was just no way out.

By the time I got to the field, everyone was already there. And, when I say everyone, I mean *everyone*. About a million kids were standing around waiting for me to make a big fool of myself.

"Hey, Frankovitch!" shouted T.J. when he saw me coming. "For a minute there, we didn't think you were going to show. What took you so long? Were your pants on fire?"

I think this was his way of calling me a liar again.

"The only thing smokin' is my pitching arm," I shot back.

Why I said that, I'll never know.

"Okay, here's what we're going to do," he said. "I brought along a catcher. And he'll be catching for both of us."

I looked over at the kid in the catcher's mask. It was Hank Grover, one of T.J.'s best friends.

"Oh, no. No way, T.J.," I protested. "If you get your own catcher, I should get my own catcher, too."

T.J. rolled his eyes. "What difference does it make who catches? The catcher isn't going to call balls or strikes. The umpires are going to do that. Besides, Frankovitch, none of your little moron friends knows *how* to catch."

Man, did that ever make me mad! Insulting my friends like that. I probably should have left right then and there. But there was one tiny little problem. He was right. None of my little moron friends *can* catch.

"Okay," T.J. continued, "here's how it'll work. We're each going to pitch ten balls. Your umpire and my umpire will stand together behind the plate. Then, as each ball is thrown, they'll decide whether it's a strike or a ball. And to make it fair, the umpires have to agree on every call. If they can't agree, the pitcher takes the whole thing over again. That sounds fair, right?"

By this time my stomach was tying itself in knots. All I wanted to do was go home.

"Yeah, I guess," I mumbled.

T.J. took a dime out of his pocket. "We'll flip to see who gets to pitch first," he said.

For a second, I saw a way out. "Oh, geez. Sorry, T.J. I guess we won't be able to have this contest after all. I never learned how to flip. I can do a somersault, but that's about it. Well, it was nice seeing you. Ta-ta."

T.J. grabbed me by the shirt. He held me while he threw the dime in the air and let it fall to the ground.

"Call it," he ordered.

I looked at the dime and started to whistle. "Here, dime…here, boy," I called.

T.J. didn't smile. "Cut the crap, Alex. I mean it. Now, I'm going to throw this up one more time and…"

I made a sick face. "You're going to throw up. Right here? Right now? That's disgusting. Really, T.J., I want no part of this."

His grip tightened on my shirt.

"Heads or tails?"

I called tails.

It was heads.

Not a good sign.

"Okay, I won the toss, so I'll go first," said T.J.

He took his ball and glove to the pitcher's mound.

T.J.'s umpire, Eddie Fowler, and my umpire, Brian, took their places behind home plate. I hated to admit it, but having two umpires really did seem pretty fair. The trouble was, it was almost *too* fair. If I was going to stand a chance, I would definitely need a little *help* from my good old pal, Brian (if you get my drift).

I called him over for a last-minute chat.

"Okay, listen, Brian," I said, "just because T.J. Stoner happens to be the best pitcher that anyone has ever seen, that doesn't mean that he's perfect. So whatever you do, don't be afraid to call any of his pitches a ball. Any pitch at all, I mean. Like even if it's right over the plate, for instance, and you just feel like saying the word *ball*…then go ahead and say *ball*. You're the umpire, right? You can say whatever you want to. And please keep in mind that I will be glad to pay you fifty cents for every ball you call."

Just then, I heard T.J.'s voice from the mound. "Hey, Alex, don't even think about getting Brian to cheat for you. I told him before you got here that if I caught him cheating, he'd go home without his head."

Brian patted my shoulder. "Sorry, Alex. But my head and I have grown sort of attached over the years."

T.J. called out again. "Okay, I'm ready! Let's go!"

I gulped. Ready? He was ready…*already?*

I yelled back. "Wait! Aren't you going to take some practice pitches first? I thought we were going to get practice pitches!"

T.J. smirked. "You can take them if you need to, Frankovitch. But I'm ready to go."

Just then, he went into his windup. Some kids look dumb when they're winding up. But I swear, T.J. looked just like Greg Maddux.

He threw.

The ball hit the catcher's mitt at about sixty miles an hour. But even worse, it hit his glove exactly in the center.

"Strike one!" shouted both umpires together.

T.J. didn't even blink. He just got ready and threw the next pitch.

"Strike two!" shouted the umpires again.

This time, T.J. looked over in my direction and smiled. I leaned down and pretended I was tying my shoe so I wouldn't have to look at him.

"What's the matter, Alex?" he said. "Is the ball flying by so fast that it untied your little sneakers?"

He threw his third pitch. Perfect, again. The guy was making me totally sick. Every single pitch he threw went whizzing directly over the plate. The catcher never even had to move a muscle. Ten straight pitches…ten straight strikes.

T.J. walked off the mound cool as anything. He tossed me the ball.

"Okay, Skinnybones. Let's see your curve," he said.

As T.J. sat down on the sidelines, Brian came over to wish me luck.

I glared at him. "What's the matter, did you forget how to say the word 'ball'?"

"Oh, get off it, Alex," he said. "All his pitches were perfect. You really didn't expect me to cheat, did you?"

I just glared at him. "I'll remember how you feel about cheating the next time I feel you tapping me on the back during a math test," I snapped.

After that, I picked up my glove and slowly walked out to the pitcher's mound. *Really* slowly, I mean. As in slow motion, practically.

The thing is, if you walk slow enough, there's always a chance that the unexpected could happen. Like a tornado could pop up and carry off the spectators, for instance. Or there could be a total eclipse of the sun, perhaps.

But unfortunately, this time nothing happened at all. When I got to the mound, there wasn't a cloud in the sky.

There was no weaseling out of it now. I took a deep breath and turned around.

My heart stopped. Geez! It was farther to home plate than I remembered! There was no way I could throw strikes from that far! No way!

The umpires lined up behind home plate, and the catcher got set.

"Are you ready yet, Skinnybones? Or do you need to practice?" yelled T.J. mockingly.

Aha! A perfect opportunity to stall for time.

I walked off the mound and headed for T.J. on the sidelines. Then I stood on my tiptoes and tried to look him in the eye.

"Okay, this name-calling has got to stop, T.J.," I said, trying to sound tough. "For your information, there is nothing *skinny* about my bones. They are just regular normal bones, okay? So I would appreciate it if you would stop calling me that stupid name."

T.J. grabbed hold of my arm and held it up next to his.

"If your bones aren't skinny," he said, "then why is my arm so much bigger than yours?"

"Your bones are chub-ettes," I told him.

T.J.'s eyes started getting real squinty. I hurried back out to the mound before he could pound me.

After that, I stood there a while trying to remember how to begin my windup.

Which do I lift first...my left leg or my right leg? And then what? Is there a hop involved? Or a skip? Or a jump?

Pretty soon some of the kids started yelling for me to get started. I swallowed hard and pulled my glove back toward my chest. Then I stared at the catcher's mitt and raised my left leg high in the air. Unfortunately, I lost my balance and started hopping all over the place.

Both of the umpires totally cracked up. The catcher fell right over in the dirt laughing.

"Time out!" I yelled. "No fair! Interference by the umpires and the catcher! They're not allowed to laugh! Laughing is very distracting!"

For once in his life, T.J. agreed with me. He went over and tried to get the three of them to calm down. But still, it took a few minutes before they finally got themselves under control.

Once again, I went into my windup. I pulled my glove back to my chest, raised my left leg high into the air, hopped around a little, and let it fly.

Well, maybe *fly* is the wrong word. Mostly what it did was bounce and skip in the dirt. But the good news was, eventually it rolled directly over the plate.

Whoa, not bad, Alex, old boy! I thought. *At least you've got it aimed in the right direction!*

"Ball one!" shouted both umpires together.

I shrugged my shoulders and walked off the mound.

"Okie-doke. Well, I guess that's it, T.J.," I said. "I lost. One little mistake on my first curve ball and it's all over. There's no way I can win now. I can't even tie. It's really a shame, too. That's probably the only bad pitch I'd have thrown all day."

T.J. grabbed me by the shirt again. "Oh, no, you don't, Frankovitch," he said. "You have nine more balls to throw. We had a deal, remember? Ten pitches. Now get back to that mound and we'll just see how good you are."

I took a deep breath. There was no sense trying to argue with him. He was going to make me do it no matter what.

Slowly I turned around and headed back.

There's still hope, Alex. Just throw it a little higher. That's all you need to do. Just a couple of good solid strikes, and you won't end up looking like a complete idiot.

My heart was beating faster than ever. I took a deep breath and got ready to throw my second pitch. My windup was the same, but something terrible happened when I started to throw. As I brought the ball behind my head, it slipped out of my fingers and rolled to second base.

The catcher fell in the dirt laughing again. Brian did, too. His mouth formed the words "Ball two," but nothing came out.

By this time I felt totally sick. All I wanted to do was get the whole thing over with so I could go home and die. I got the ball, wound up again, and threw my third pitch as hard as I could.

T.J. was watching from the sidelines. The ball hit him smack in the forehead.

What d'ya know...my old bean ball was back.

I couldn't keep from grinning. "STRIKE ONE!" I shouted out.

T.J. ran out to the mound and gave me a shove. "What do you mean, strike one?"

I pointed at the red bump forming on his head. "Well, it *struck* you, didn't it?" I asked.

T.J. shoved me again. "Yeah? Well, let's see how *you* like being struck, Skinnybones," he said.

Then he punched my arm as hard as he could. And he kept doing it again and again. Right in the same spot.

"Just remember what this feels like the next time you think about hitting someone with a baseball," he said.

My arm was killing me, but in a way I felt sort of flattered. T.J. actually thought I had been aiming for his head and had hit my target. I mean, when you

47

think about it, it was a pretty nice compliment.

Anyway, it was clear by now: the contest was over. I couldn't have pitched again if I'd wanted to. My arm hung limp at my side like it had croaked or something. I checked to see if it was bleeding, but no such luck. I hate that, by the way. When something hurts as bad as my arm did, the least it could do is bleed a little.

As T.J. walked away from the field, his friends followed him. Most of them were patting him on the shoulder and raving about what a great pitcher he was.

If anyone had patted *my* shoulder, my entire arm would have fallen right off into the dirt.

I looked around for Brian, but he had already started walking home without me. At first that made me mad, but I guess he was just too embarrassed to walk home with a loser.

In a way, I couldn't blame him.

I didn't want to walk home with me, either.

chapter seven

HARD-BOILED EGGHEAD

Sometimes I wonder why I even bother to play baseball at all. I hate the uniforms, I can't throw, and I don't like playing right field. Lately I've been giving this a lot of thought, and there's only one thing I can come up with...

I play for the caps.

Baseball caps are probably the greatest invention of all time. No matter what you look like, as soon as you put on a baseball cap you automatically look like a ballplayer. A *real* ballplayer, I mean. Like Bobby Bonds, or Ken Griffey, Jr. or Cal Ripken. I'm not kidding. Even my cat looks a little like Ripken with a cap on.

Once—just to prove my theory—I did a baseball cap experiment with my grandmother. My grandmother's about eighty years old, but she doesn't look it. She doesn't need a cane or anything, and she only wears glasses when she reads.

One of the things I like best about my grandmother is her blue hair. It sort of reminds me of cotton candy. I'm not sure that she really knows it's blue, though. A few months ago, at Sunday dinner, she told my mother that she puts a "steel gray" rinse on it. I started to tell her that it looked more like "robin's-egg blue," but my mother shoved a roll in my mouth.

Anyway, after we finished eating, I snuck up to my room and grabbed my baseball cap. Then I crept up behind my grandmother and put it on her head.

Aha! Just as I had always suspected! She was a dead ringer for Tino Martinez!

Grandma wasn't a very good sport about it. She yanked my cap off her head and threw it on the floor.

Man, was her blue hair ever a mess! Now she looked like Don King, that boxing promoter guy. I tried to help her smooth it, but she swatted my hand away. Not before I noticed the bald spot, though. Right at the top of her head, Grandma had a little bald spot.

I offered to let her put my cap on to hide it, but she left the table in a huff. I knew exactly how she felt. My barber, Mr. Peoples, has given me more bald spots than I can even count.

I'll never forget the time he made my head look like a cue ball. Looking back, it was probably my own fault, though. As soon as I walked in his shop that day, it was obvious that Mr. Peoples was not in a good mood. And it's a well-known fact that when barbers are feeling down, they give kids funny haircuts to cheer themselves up.

That's why I always try to find out how Mr. Peoples is feeling before I sit down in the chair. But on this particular day, it didn't do me any good at all.

"Hello, Mr. Peoples," I said pleasantly. "How are you feeling today? Arthritis acting up? Problems with the wife?"

Mr. Peoples frowned. "Get in the chair, Alex. I'm tired. My feet hurt. And I'm not in the mood for your jokes."

Right away, I started backing out of his shop.

"Okie-doke. Well, nice chatting with you, Mr. P. I think I hear my mother calling me from the parking lot. I'll come back another day when your feet are feeling better."

Mr. Peoples pointed to the chair. "Sit!" he ordered.

Mr. Peoples has known me since I was two, so he feels comfortable bossing me around like that.

I hesitated. "I don't know, Mr. Peoples. Are you sure? I mean, are you positive you want me to sit down? Because if you're upset about something, I would be happy to leave you alone to gather your thoughts."

This time, his face got totally red. "I said *sit!*" he blustered.

Nervously, I climbed into the big vinyl seat. A man holding scissors is not a man to mess with.

"Well, okay then, Mr. Peoples. But I really don't need a big haircut today. Mostly all I need is a little trim. Just a little bit off the sides and that's all."

Mr. Peoples didn't hear a word I said. He was too busy plugging in his electric clippers.

"No, wait, Mr. Peoples," I said quickly. "I really don't think you'll be needing the clippers today. I just need a trim, remember?"

His mood wasn't getting better. "Who's the barber here, Alex, you or me?"

That's when I decided to be quiet. If there was one thing I didn't want to do, it was to make the guy any grouchier than he already was.

Mr. Peoples took his scissors and began snipping at my hair. No, wait…snipping is the wrong word. The word is *hacking*. Mr. Peoples started *hacking* at my hair.

"Whoa, you're really going to town there, aren't you, Mr. P.? It's getting kinda short, don't you think?" I asked.

That's when Mr. Peoples picked up the clippers and began buzzing all around the back of my head. Before I had a chance to protest, he was already heading up toward my left ear.

Then all of a sudden, he stopped cold.

"Whoopsie!" he said.

My stomach turned over inside of me. Of all the words you don't ever want to hear your barber say, *whoopsie* is right at the top of the list.

"*Whoopsie?* Did you say *'whoopsie,'* Mr. Peoples? *Whoopsie,* as in a mistake has just occurred up there?"

I looked in the mirror and turned my head. That's when I saw the "whoopsie." It was a large round bald spot right over my left ear.

Mr. Peoples brushed the area lightly with his fingers. "Looks like this haircut might be a little bit shorter than you wanted it, Alex. But at least it will be nice and cool for the summer."

My eyes opened wide. "The summer?" I said. "The summer? This is March, Mr. Peoples. The summer is still months away."

Mr. Peoples nudged me with his elbow and grinned. "That's my point...get it? Even months from now, this haircut will still be nice and cool."

He began to chuckle. Already he had cheered himself up a ton.

He started the clippers again.

"More?" I asked, feeling sick.

"Well, we can't leave her like this, can we?" he said. "Gotta even her up. Right?"

I couldn't stand to look anymore, so I covered my eyes with my hands and waited until he was finished. After circling my head with the clippers about twenty more times, he finally shut them off.

Slowly I opened my eyes. No! It couldn't be! My hair was gone! *Totally* gone, I mean! I looked like a hard-boiled egg with a face!

Mr. Peoples dusted the hair off my neck. "Well? What do you think?"

I could barely speak. "What do I think about what?"

"About your hair. What do you think about your hair?" he asked cheerfully.

Stunned, I gazed at my hair lying all over the floor. "I think it looked better on my head. *That's* what I think."

Mr. Peoples chuckled some more as he got the broom to sweep it up.

I panicked. "No! Wait! Don't!" I shouted. Then I jumped down from the chair and started picking up hair clumps and trying to stick them back on my head. I stuffed the rest in my pocket for later re-attachment.

Mr. Peoples laughed again. By now he was a regular jolly old elf.

"You kill me, boy!" he roared. Then he held out his hand for the money.

I slapped ten dollars down on the counter and ran home as fast as I could. My mother met me at the door.

"LOOK WHAT THAT MAN DID TO ME!" I yelled, pointing to my head. "HE'S INSANE, I TELL YOU! *INSANE!*"

Mom covered her mouth with her hand. It was clear that she was trying not to laugh in my face.

"The good thing about hair is that it always grows back," she managed to say.

"Yeah, well, that might be the good thing about hair, Mother," I snapped, "but exactly what is the good thing about…NO HAIR?!"

Finally, my mother started to lose it and hurried out of the room.

"No! Don't go! I need help here!" I called.

A minute later, she was back wearing sunglasses. "I apologize. But the glare coming off your head was blinding," she said with a straight face.

"Not funny, Mom!" I blurted. "Not funny!"

That's when I remembered it! My baseball cap! I had to find my baseball cap!

I flew down the hall to my room. *Please! Please! Just let it be where I can find it,* I prayed.

I opened up my closet door. Yes! For once I had remembered to put it back on the hook where it belonged.

Quickly, I put it on my head. It fell down over my eyes. But after adjusting the back strap, I looked in the mirror. Almost at once, I started to settle down. What a relief! I looked like a cross between Mark Grace and David Justice.

I'm telling you, baseball caps are the invention of the century.

Now, if only baseball caps could make me hit home runs like David Justice, everything would be perfect.

I guess you could say that hitting a home run is a dream of mine. I don't think it will ever come true, though. It's pretty hard to hit a home run when all you can do is bunt.

Bunt. I've always thought that was such a stupid word. The first time I heard it I was only about seven. This kid on my baseball team was on his way up to bat. And before he left the bench, he turned around and said to me, "I think I'm going to bunt."

At first, I had no idea what he was talking about.

But whatever it was, it didn't sound good. I sat there and sat there trying to figure it out. And then out of nowhere, it clicked.

Bunt? Wait a second! I bet it's another word for "puke"!

Oh, no! That poor kid's sick and no one knows it but me!

Quickly, I got off the bench and ran over to the coach. "Coach! Coach! I think Danny Patrillo is going to start bunting any minute!" I said frantically.

The coach nodded calmly. "That's okay, Alex," he said. "Don't worry about it. I told him to bunt."

Okay. Now I was *really* confused. Why in the world would a coach tell one of his players to hurl? Was this some strange baseball rule I hadn't heard of? Were you allowed to throw up and run to first? Was he hoping to catch the other team off guard or something?

Oh, geez, I hoped he wouldn't tell me to bunt, too!

I tugged on his shirt. "Listen, Coach," I said, "I don't think I could bunt even if I wanted to. I feel very good today. Plus I haven't even eaten dinner yet."

The coach looked at me kind of strange and told me to sit down. I went back to the bench and watched the kid at bat. When the ball came, he took his bat and held it sideways in front of him. I figured he was just trying to get it out of the way so he wouldn't bunt on it. And since I was next at bat, I thought this was a very considerate thing to do.

But, instead of getting sick, the kid took the bat and tapped the ball toward third base. Then he ran as fast as he could and made it to first in plenty of time.

"Great!" yelled the coach. "Great bunt, Danny!"

I nudged the kid next to me. "I didn't see it. I didn't see him bunt. Did he do it in the grass? Where is it?"

"Where is what?" he asked.

"You know," I said. "The *bunt*. Where is the *bunt*?"

"Weren't you watching?" he asked. "He bunted the ball down the third-base line and then ran to first."

Suddenly, I knew what a bunt really was. Man, did I ever feel like an idiot! Thank goodness no one ever knew what I had been talking about.

Anyway, from that day on, I started working on my bunting. It just seemed like the perfect skill for a kid my size. And now, after four years of practice, I'm probably one of the best bunters in the entire Little League. It's not the kind of thing that gets you any respect. But still, it's something.

Sometimes Brian helps me practice my bunting at recess. Last week, T.J. saw us and came strolling over again.

"Bunting is for wimps," he announced loudly.

I ignored him.

"Any kid with a half a muscle can hit the ball for real," he said.

Still, I ignored him.

"Ooops...I forgot. You don't have half a muscle, do you, Skinnybones?" he said.

He grinned meanly. "Hey, I just thought of something. Only *runts* bunt! Get it? Get it, Alex? I made a poem!"

That's when I decided to stop ignoring him.

Brian tossed me another ball. I held the bat steady until the very last minute. Then I turned it sharply and directed the ball right into T.J.'s head.

"Whoa! Sorry, T.J.!" I said. "Man, it seems that all I've been doing lately is accidentally hitting you with baseballs. Geez, it's a good thing they keep hitting you in the skull. Otherwise, you could get hurt."

For the millionth time in my life, T.J. shoved me to the ground again and sat on top of me.

He was smirking like crazy. "We'll just see how

good you bunt on Saturday, funny guy," he said.

For a second I didn't know what he was talking about. Then, all of a sudden, I remembered. Saturday was the day when our Little League teams were scheduled to play each other.

Wonderful. And now I'd gone and made him mad.

I closed my eyes. *Way to go, Alex. You've done it again.*

chapter eight
A FACEFUL OF FLAKES

Usually, when I go to the Little League field for a game, I don't know who we're going to play until I get there. I just go to the game, lose, and go home. The way I look at it, losing is losing. Who cares who you lose *to?*

A lot of kids don't feel that way, though. T.J. Stoner is one of them. T.J. always knows exactly which team he's going up against. Then, a couple of days before the game, he goes around school announcing how badly the other team is going to get whipped. Nobody ever argues with him, either. 'Cause they all know it's true.

Anyway, that's why I wasn't surprised when T.J. went through the halls bragging about how Franklin's Sporting Goods was going to "mop up the floor" with Fran and Ethel's Cleaning Service.

Fran and Ethel's Cleaning Service—that's the name of my team this year. Catchy, huh? When I first found out about it, I thought about quitting. But my dad said that Fran and Ethel had paid a lot of money to sponsor our team, and it wouldn't be fair if everyone quit just because it was a stupid name.

So far, I've never had a team name that sounds as neat as Franklin's Sporting Goods. Last year my team was called Preston's Pest Control. Our team banner had a roach being knocked out with a baseball bat. It was totally humiliating.

Anyway, on Friday morning, right after class started, T.J. raised his hand and made another public announcement.

"Tomorrow, at 10:30 A.M., my Little League team is going to be playing Alex's team. So I was thinking some of you guys might want to come by the field and watch us play."

My stomach turned over. Oh, geez, no! He was inviting the entire class? No way! My team hadn't won a game all season, and T.J.'s was in first place. It was going to be a slaughter!

Quickly, I jumped up. "Why?" I called out.

My teacher looked at me strangely. "Why what, Alex?"

"Why would anyone want to come to our game?"

Desperately, I looked around the room. "Don't you people have lives of your own? It's just a stupid Little League game."

T.J. smiled broadly. "Well, not exactly. There's something else you guys should probably know. I don't want to brag, but I'm going to be pitching tomorrow. And if I win the game, I'll set a Little League pitching record for most games won in a row."

He paused so that his thrilling information could sink in.

"It'll put me in all the record books," he added.

Mrs. Grayson's whole face lit up. "Really, T.J.? That's terrific!"

I jumped up again. "Books, schmooks! Record, schmecord!" I hollered.

Mrs. Grayson told me to be quiet. But T.J. wouldn't quit. He kept talking about that stupid game all day long.

Even after the bell rang and kids were leaving the room, he stood at the door issuing personal invitations. "You're gonna be there, right?" he'd ask. "You're not going to let me down, are you?"

I tried to duck past him, but he grabbed my shirt. Then he pulled me right up to his face and smirked.

"See you tomorrow, *Alexandra*," he said.

I wrinkled my nose at his breath. "Phew.

Mackerel for lunch again?" I asked.

But T.J. just laughed. "We'll see how funny you are tomorrow when the whole class turns up to watch you lose. Loser."

Then he sort of rubbed his hands together and walked away.

Man, was I ever in for it now. This was even worse than the pitching contest. If there's one thing worse than losing, it's losing in front of your whole entire class!

I've never even played in front of a crowd before. With a team like mine, a lot of the parents don't even show up. In fact, so far there are only two people that have been at every single game we've played this year.

Fran and Ethel.

They always come to watch us play right after they get off from work. You can tell who they are because they usually wring out their mops while we warm up.

It wasn't surprising that I couldn't eat any dinner that night. And I didn't sleep at all. Mostly, I just lay in bed trying to think of a way to get out of playing. I must have gone through a hundred plans before I finally came up with one that I thought might work.

It was pretty extreme. But it was my only chance.

The next morning, I made sure my parents were at the breakfast table. Then I dragged myself into the kitchen on my stomach and slowly pulled myself over to the table.

"'Morning," I said weakly.

My father looked down at me. "'Morning, Alex," he said back.

"'Morning," said Mom. "What kind of cereal do you want?"

Feebly, I raised my head. "Cornflakes. I'll have a few cornflakes, please," I muttered.

My mother got up from the table and stepped over me to get to the refrigerator.

"Juice?" she asked.

I nodded. What was *wrong* with these people? Didn't they notice that I was lying on the floor?

Mom bent down and put my bowl in front of me. "You'd better hurry and eat," she said. "You have to get ready for your game soon."

Okay. Fine. I didn't know what little game they were playing here, but I could play right along.

Leaving the cereal on the floor, I pulled myself into my chair. I made a big deal of it, grunting and groaning all the way.

"I think I'd like to eat up here," I said, trying to catch my breath. "Could someone please get me my cornflakes and juice?"

My parents glanced down at the bowl on the floor.

"You should have brought it up here with you, son," said Dad. "Your mother and I are eating right now."

For the next few seconds, I sat there tapping my fingers on the table. Then, even slower than before, I leaned down until my hands were touching the floor again. The chair flipped over on me as I dropped back down. But Mom and Dad still didn't react.

This called for drastic action. Something so outrageous they couldn't ignore it. That's when I started eating right out of the bowl. Without a *spoon,* I mean. Like Fluffy.

My mother looked down and dropped a napkin on my head.

That did it!

"Hey! What kind of parents are you, anyway?" I hollered. "Your pathetic little son is lying on the floor, eating like an animal, and all you can do is drop a napkin on his head? Don't you even want to know what happened to me?"

"We already know," said my mother.

"You mean you already know that in the middle of the night, Fluffy jumped up on my bed…and the big oaf went to sleep on my legs…and she cut off the circulation to my entire lower body…which is why my feet and legs are asleep and I can't stand up? You already know all *that?*"

"No, Alex," said Mom. "We know that you're trying to get out of going to your game today. Brian's parents called this morning and said that most of your class will be there. So we figured you'd be pulling some kind of stunt to get to stay home."

I rolled over.

"Oh."

After that, I just lay there. For a really long time, I mean. I just lay there staring up at the ceiling.

Finally, I rolled back on my stomach again and silently pulled myself back out of the kitchen. Sometimes, when you're caught doing something stupid, it's less humiliating if you just ease out of it gracefully.

When I got back to my room, I stood up and put on my uniform.

My pants fell down again.

This was going to be the worst day of my life.

chapter nine

LOSERS PLAY BALL...
FILM AT ELEVEN

I put on a belt and headed over to the baseball field. The Little League uses the same field as the middle school. It's not far from my house. But this time, as I turned the corner, I froze dead in my tracks.

The bleachers were packed! And when I say packed, I mean packed solid!

My skin broke out in a cold sweat. No! This couldn't be happening! Why would all those people show up at a dumb Little League game? It didn't make sense. Even if my entire class showed up, the bleachers wouldn't come close to being filled. There had to be a mistake somewhere. The middle school was having some kind of function, I bet.

That's when it hit me.

Wait! Hold it! It's June, Alex! June! June, as in Graduation Day!

Of course! The eighth-grade class was graduating. And there had been a mix-up in the schedules. Someone had forgotten to tell the Little League.

I looked up to the sky and folded my hands. "Thank you, God. Thank you, thank you! This is a wonderful thing you've done here! A wonderful, Godly, zippy, wonderful thing!"

Relieved, I sat down on the curb to wait for my parents. They'd be coming along soon, and I wanted to be the first one to break the good news.

As I was waiting there, a truck from Channel Six News pulled up and a cameraman got out. He lifted some heavy equipment out of the back door.

"Are you guys going to be filming that graduation ceremony over there?" I asked.

The man didn't pay much attention to me. "What graduation? That's a baseball game," he mumbled.

All of a sudden, the cold sweat was back.

Okay. Okay. Don't panic. There's a reasonable explanation here, Alex. Nothing to get excited about.

I swallowed hard. "A baseball game? Like what kind of baseball game? Like the middle school championship game, do you mean? 'Cause that would make sense, because I mean the crowd is huge."

The cameraman shook his head. "Nope. It's not a championship. It's just a regular Saturday morning Little League game. In fact, somebody told me that one of the teams hasn't won a game all season. What losers, huh?"

I collapsed on the sidewalk. Just flat out collapsed.

The cameraman glanced down. "You okay, kid?"

I opened one eye and stared up at him.

"Okay?" I asked. "Am I okay? No. I am *not* okay. That's my team you're talking about, mister. It's my team that hasn't won a game all year. What kind of man are you, anyway? What kind of man would want to embarrass a pathetic Little League team by showing them lose on the six o'clock news?"

"Whoa! Wait a minute, son. Calm down," he said. "I'm not here to embarrass anyone. It's the *other* team we're interested in. The one with that hotshot pitcher on it."

I threw down my cap. "T.J.! I knew it! I knew this was his fault! He probably called the station, didn't he? He probably called the station and invited you here personally!"

The man shrugged. "I don't know who set it up, kid. The story was headline news in the paper this morning, though. That probably explains all the people. It said this kid has won every single Little

League game he's ever played in. If his team wins today, it will be his 125th straight winning game. That's quite a string," he said.

I closed my eyes. "String, schming," I muttered miserably.

I got to my feet and started walking.

Desperately, I looked into the sky again. "God? Remember a few minutes ago when I was thanking you? Well, it was my understanding that you'd done a little miracle for me or something. But now it turns out you didn't. And so I think it would be a nice gesture on your part if you could make it up to me."

I racked my brain for a plan.

"Okay…got it. Just make the people in the bleachers go home. You could do that, couldn't you, God? Just make everyone think they left the water running in their bathtubs. That would be easy enough, right? It might even be kind of amusing, don't you think?"

I looked around to see if anyone was leaving. People were still piling into the stands.

"Okay, then how about this?" I bargained. "Just make the cameraman go home. Just that one little man, God. If the cameraman goes home, I will go to Sunday school every single Sunday for the rest of my life without a fight. I promise."

I turned around. The cameraman was walking

behind me, carrying his equipment to the field.

"All right. This is it...my last idea. And this is something right up your alley, God. A lightning bolt. Close enough to scare them...but far enough away not to hurt anyone. Just one tiny little lightning bolt, God, and I promise I will run home this very minute and read my entire book of Bible stories from cover to cover."

I looked into the sky. It was the sunniest day since my pitching contest.

My shoulders dropped even lower than before. I hung my head. God is not the pushover that some people would like you to believe.

When I finally arrived at the field, my team was already out there warming up. I could see the tension in their faces. It was obvious I wasn't the only one who was sick about this.

I headed out to right field. My knees were shaking underneath me.

"Hey, Frankovitch! Where in the heck have you been?" shouted my coach. "I thought we were going to have to play without a right fielder! Get out there and warm up! Now hustle!"

I began to trot.

"All right, Alex. Okay. That's far enough," hollered my coach again. "I'm going to hit you a couple out there. Now get ready."

He hit me a high pop fly. I was nervous as anything. All those eyes in the bleachers. I could actually feel them staring at me. But the ball came so fast, I didn't have time to dwell on it. I'd watched the ball leave the bat, followed it in the air, and caught it.

Perfect! A perfect catch!

My nerves settled a little. Geez. Maybe this wasn't going to be so tough, after all. Maybe a crowd brought out the best in me or something.

"Okay, Alex. Here comes another one."

This time it was a grounder. As soon as I saw it coming, I ran up to it, bent down, and scooped it up in my glove.

"Hey! All right out there, Alex!" yelled the coach. "Way to play!"

Man, did he ever sound relieved.

My shoulders relaxed.

I looked up to the sky and smiled.

chapter ten
WHO'S ON SECOND?

The umpire called to the coaches. It was time for the game to begin.

On the sideline, T.J. was being interviewed for the six o'clock news. I tried to get close enough to listen, but they'd already finished. As T.J. walked off, I heard the interviewer say, "Good luck out there today, T.J. We're all rooting for you."

I looked into the bleachers and saw Fran and Ethel. They were hard to spot because they didn't have their mops with them. But the two of them got my attention and gave me a thumbs-up sign. I smiled. *Not everyone's rooting for you, T.J.*

T.J.'s team was the home team, so they hustled onto the field. Meanwhile, T.J. started warming up on the mound. Just like in our pitching contest, every warm-up pitch he threw went zinging over the plate at about sixty miles an hour.

"Batter up!" shouted the ump.

Kevin Murphy was the first batter on our team. Kevin can hit the ball a ton when he connects. The trouble is, he mostly doesn't. *Connect,* I mean.

As soon as he stepped up to the plate, I could tell he was really nervous. He kept trying to spit, but nothing would come out. Instead, he just kept making this funny sound with his lips...like *puh... puh...puh*. It was pretty awful.

T.J. grinned. Then he wound up and threw the ball as hard as he could.

"Steeerrriiiikkke one!" yelled the umpire.

Kevin looked confused. "Did we start already?" he asked the ump.

T.J. went into his windup for the second pitch. This time he threw it a little slower. Just as the ball got to the plate, it curved.

Kevin swung with all his might.

"Steeerrriiiikkke two!" yelled the umpire again.

Poor Kevin. I really felt sorry for him. Whenever you swing as hard as you can and miss, you always feel like a fool. He tried acting cool, but it didn't work. When he knocked the dirt off his shoes, he accidentally hit himself in the ankle.

Embarrassed, he quickly got ready to bat again.

Unfortunately, the third pitch that T.J. threw was even better than the first two. Kevin just watched it go whizzing by.

"Strike three! Batter's out!" called the ump.

Everyone in the stands began to cheer loudly for T.J.

Kevin stood there stunned for a second. Then he walked over and sat down on the bench, bent over so no one could see his face, and began to cry. It wasn't the kind of crying you could hear. But you could see his back heaving up and down, so you definitely knew he was sobbing.

At first the whole team was pretty embarrassed about it. But as it turned out, Kevin was the best batter of the inning. He was the only one who swung. The second batter, Willy Jenson, just stood there, counted three pitches, and sat down. And the third batter never even took the bat off his shoulder.

Our team was out in the field before we knew it. Everyone was looking totally depressed. It was pretty clear that we needed something to get the old team spirit going.

I called them into a huddle for a pep talk.

"Okay, you guys," I said. "All we need to do is hold 'em. What do you say? Let's get them out one-two-three! Three up. Three down!"

Densel Johnson, the first baseman, laughed right

in my face. "Are you nuts, Alex? Our team hasn't made three outs in a row all year."

"Yeah, Frankovitch. What are you trying to do? *Mock* us? We'll be lucky if we make three outs the entire game," said Willy Jenson.

So much for team spirit.

I didn't care what those guys said, though. I was still determined to cheer our team on.

Frankie Rogers was our starting pitcher. As I walked to right field, I watched him warm up. Frankie only throws two warm-up pitches per game. He says he doesn't have that many good pitches in him, and he doesn't want to risk using them up in practice.

I started chattering from the outfield. "Okay, Frankie, pitch it in there, babe. Right over the plate, Frankie! You can do it! You can do it, Frankie babe."

Frankie threw the first pitch. It hit the dirt about ten feet in front of the plate.

"Ball one!" shouted the umpire.

"That's okay, Frankie, don't worry. You can do it!" I yelled. "Chuck it in there, Frankie! Smoke it in there, guy!"

Just then, Frankie made the time-out sign and began walking toward right field. I figured he wanted to have some sort of strategy session, so I ran up to meet him.

"Would you please shut up, Alex?" he said. "How am I supposed to concentrate with all that noise out there? You're just adding pressure. That's all you're doing."

"No, Frankie. I'm *encouraging* you," I explained. "It's baseball chatter. I'm supposed to chatter. The whole team is supposed to chatter."

Frankie rolled his eyes. "Get a clue, Alex. This is not a normal game. And we are not a normal team. And I do not respond well to *chatter*. So put a sock in it, okay?"

Frankie stomped back to the pitcher's mound. His next pitch hit the batter on the foot and he took his base. The batter after that got hit in the arm.

The whole thing was totally humiliating. It was bad enough that Frankie was hitting people. But he wasn't even throwing the ball hard enough for it to hurt anyone. The guys weren't even blinking.

I shook my head and glanced over to the sidelines. That's when I saw the cameraman. He had just spotted me in the field. And he was pointing his camera in my direction!

Oh, geez! Oh, no! He said he would only be filming T.J.!

Quickly, I put both my hands over my face so that no one would recognize me on the news.

Unfortunately, just as I covered my eyes, I heard

the loud crack of the bat.

Somebody had hit the ball...*hard!*

I looked up. A kid was running to first base, and all the guys on my team had turned to stare at right field. Right field? Wait...that was me!

A pop fly was headed my way! And I didn't even know where it was!

Quickly, I looked up into the sky, but the sun was directly in my eyes! I was doomed! I was finished! I was dead meat! Any second a hard ball was going to smack me right in the head, and I had no idea where it was even coming from!

I had to do something to protect myself!

In a flash, I took my glove off my hand and put it on my head.

THUD!

The ball hit my glove! Then it rolled off the top of my head and landed on the ground next to me!

Frankie Rogers started going nuts. "He dropped it! He dropped the stupid ball!" he screamed.

Man, did that make me mad. Frankie Rogers, of all people! Yelling at *me* for making a mistake!

"I did not!" I shouted back at him. "How can a person drop something when he didn't even catch it in the first place? Just because something lands on your head does not mean that you caught it!"

"It does too!" shouted Frankie. "You caught it on

your head, and then you dropped it!"

Man, was I ticked. I kicked at my glove.

"If a bird poops on your head, you don't say that you've caught it, do you, you jerk?" I yelled.

Unfortunately, I was so busy yelling, I had totally forgotten about the ball. By the time I threw it in, two runs had scored and the batter was safe at third.

I looked at the sidelines. My coach was waving at me.

Odd, I thought. But just to be polite, I waved back.

"He's not waving, Frankovitch, you moron!" shouted Ricki Delaney, the center fielder. "He's shaking his fist!"

I squinted my eyes and looked closer. Yup. That was a fist, all right. The guy was furious. For the first time in my life, I was actually grateful to be out in right field.

It took a few minutes for things to settle back down. But finally, Frankie got ready to face his fourth batter.

Slowly, old T.J. Stoner walked up to the plate and took a few practice swings. Then he spit in his hands, grinned, and pointed at me with his bat.

Panicked, I began backing up. No. Please. No. If I dropped another one, I was done for.

Frankie pitched the ball.

T.J. leaned back and swung it with all his might. It was a hard grounder, and it was screaming my way! It streaked past the first baseman and tore into right field!

Stay calm, Alex! Stay calm! Just do what you did in practice today! You can do it! You can get T.J. Stoner out!

I did everything right. I swear I did. First, I ran up to meet the ball. Then I stooped down to block it. And I didn't take my eye off it. Not even for a split second!

It's almost here! I've got it! I've got it!

But just as the ball was about to roll into my glove, it hit a clump of grass and took a crazy bounce to the right.

"NO!" I screamed.

I made a diving leap, but it was no use. The ball sped away and rolled all the way to the back fence.

The crowd went wild. T.J. was on his way to an inside-the-park home run. And he wasn't even hurrying. I watched him as he rounded second base. He looked over his shoulder at me and tipped his cap. Man, did he make me sick!

Once again, I had completely forgotten about the ball. It didn't matter, though. I couldn't have thrown it all the way home even if I'd wanted to.

Ricki Delaney finally threw it in. But T.J. was already safe.

By now my coach's face was so red he looked like a chili pepper. For a minute, I actually thought he might explode. I needed help...*big time.*

I looked up to the clouds. "Please, God, please.... whatever you do, do not—I repeat, do *not*—let our team get up to bat again until my coach settles down. If I have to go in now, he will kill me, God. I know he will. And if you think I'm a problem down here, just imagine what it would be like to have me running around up there with you. You'd never have a minute's peace, God. Think about it."

Right after that, Frankie Rogers threw nine strikes in a row.

I looked up again. "I've done something to upset you, haven't I, God? You're still mad about me wearing a gorilla suit in last year's Christmas play, aren't you?"

There was no more stalling. I had to go in.

My coach still hadn't taken his eyes off of me. He had a scary grin on his face, and he was pounding his fist into his hand.

I kept my head down and raised my eyes. "Someday we'll all look back on this and have a good chuckle," I muttered as I passed by.

"Ohhhh, believe me, Alex," he growled through

clenched teeth, "you and I are going to have a whole lot of chuckles right after the game. But right now you're up. So get your butt over there."

My heart stopped. "Up? No, Coach! How can I be up? I don't bat fourth! I never bat cleanup!"

The coach pointed. Davy Washington, our cleanup hitter, was being led off the field. "Stomach problems" was all the coach would say.

Meanwhile, the guy who usually bats fifth was all doubled over on the bench. He was breathing into a brown paper bag.

My legs felt like rubber. But somehow I managed to put on a batting helmet and head in the direction of the batter's box.

In the stands, Fran and Ethel were cheering…

On the sidelines, the camera was still rolling…

And on the mound, T.J. Stoner was grinning his head off.

This was easily the most terrifying moment of my life. There was no escape. None. No joke would save me now.

I stepped up to the plate. As I did, T.J. turned and hollered to the rest of his team. "EASY OUT! EASY OUT!"

In unison, the entire infield took four giant steps in. I swear it was almost like they had rehearsed it.

"GET READY FOR A BUNT!" yelled T.J. again.

"Great. Perfect. Give my strategy away, why don't you?" I muttered. But I didn't have a choice. It was either bunt the ball or not connect at all.

T.J. threw his first pitch.

"Steeerrriiiikkke one!" shouted the umpire.

I turned and looked at him.

"Why do umpires always yell 'strike' so loud, do you think?" I asked. "Whenever it's a ball, you guys practically whisper. But as soon as you see a strike, man, you belt it out for the whole world to hear. Why *is* that?"

The umpire told me to *watch myself, pal*.

I turned and got ready for the next pitch. I had already made up my mind. I wasn't going to just stand there and let another ball go by. If I was going to strike out, I was going to do it swinging. Or, in my case, *bunting*.

T.J. wound up and threw again. I stuck out my bat and got ready. As the ball whizzed over the plate, I bunted it sharply down the first baseline.

I took off running!

I couldn't believe it! I'd actually made contact with a T.J. Stoner pitch!

Now if only I could get on base! If I could get on base, all my problems would be over! I'd be a hero! And no one can be mad at a hero. Not even my coach.

The first baseman ran like crazy to get the ball. Meanwhile, T.J. sped over to cover first.

My teammates were screaming their lungs out! I just had to make it!

The first baseman picked up the ball and got ready to make the toss.

I was almost there! Just three more steps to go!

The toss came. T.J. reached out his glove for the catch!

He had to miss it! He just *had* to!

I flung my arms all around. "BOOGA BOOGA!" I screamed in his face. "BOOGA BOOGA!"

T.J. looked shocked. For just an instant he took his eye off the ball. And that's all it took! It shot right past him, and rolled into the outfield.

I WAS SAFE AT FIRST!

But wait!

The coach was waving me on!

As the right fielder scrambled for the ball, I headed for second.

"Legs, don't fail me now!" I yelled as I hit full speed. I didn't look back until I was safely on the bag.

The crowd in the stands went totally nuts. Fran and Ethel practically ran onto the field. This was the proudest moment of my life!

"I DID IT! I DID IT!" I screamed. "I MADE IT TO SECOND! ME! ALEX FRANKOVITCH! I'M ON SECOND BASE!"

The second baseman told me to shut up. But no one could ruin this moment for me! Not the second baseman! Not T.J. Stoner! Not anyone!

I was waving my cap to the crowd when I first saw T.J.'s coach. He ran onto the field and began yelling at the umpire. Then the next thing I knew, my coach was out there, too.

I had no idea what they could be arguing about. The play had been so simple. I had bunted…T.J. had missed it…and I had ended up on second. I still couldn't believe it! Wow! I started jumping up and down on the bag.

Suddenly, I saw the umpire walking toward me. He did not look happy.

Okay, don't panic, Alex. Maybe he's not really coming to second base at all. Maybe during the excitement, someone threw toilet paper streamers onto the outfield, and the umpire's walking out there to clean them up.

But a few seconds later, the umpire stopped right next to me. Then he leaned right down in my face and screamed, "YOU'RE OUT!"

My mouth fell wide open. "Out? How could I be out? I bunted!"

"You interfered with the play at first base," he said.

"I did not! I didn't even *touch* T.J.!"

"You put your hands in his face and shouted 'booga booga,'" said the umpire. "I call that interference. Not to mention unsportsmanlike conduct."

Just then, my coach ran up behind the umpire and handed him the rule book. "Show me!" he demanded. "Show me where it says you can't say 'booga booga!' Where is it, huh? What page is the 'no booga booga' rule on?"

I don't know why, but all of a sudden this whole conversation sounded unbelievably funny to me. I started to chuckle to myself.

The umpire told me to get off the field.

I looked up at him and grinned. "Booga," I said softly.

The man looked at me like I was nuts. And who knows? Maybe I was.

"I said, 'Get off the field,'" he repeated.

I took his hand and shook it, *very sportsmanlike*.

"Booga booga," I said again. Then, slowly, I began trotting off the field toward the bench.

Out of the corner of my eye, I could see T.J. He was laughing his head off.

Instantly, I changed direction. Now, instead of

running off the field, I began running straight toward T.J.

If he wanted to laugh, I might as well give him something even *more* to laugh about.

When I got to the mound, I lifted up his arm and started tickling him. "Wanna laugh, T.J.? This'll make you laugh," I said.

T.J. swatted at me with his cap. "Quit it, Alex! Knock it off! Everyone is watching!"

For the first time in his life, he looked embarrassed. Truly *humiliated,* I mean. It was great, too. Almost as great as getting to second base.

It didn't last long, though. The umpire had started to come after me again, so it was definitely time to split.

I gave T.J. a final tickle. Then I ran right off the field and out the gate. I didn't slow down until I was home in my own room.

I locked the door behind me and collapsed on the floor.

I had a feeling I wouldn't be coming out for a long, long time.

chapter eleven

WAKE ME WHEN I'M GROWN

I'd been in my room about an hour when I heard my parents come home from the game. I had pushed my dresser over in front of the door so that no one could get in. I wasn't sure exactly what my dad was going to do when he got home, but I was positive there would be a lecture involved. And I already knew what he'd say.

He'd start off by telling me that *running away from a problem never solves anything*. Then he'd say it was *high time* I stopped trying to make fun of everything I'm no good at. *Not everything in life is a big joke*, he would say. Then he'd end by telling me that no matter what I do in life, *I should always give a hundred and ten percent*.

After that, he'd stare at me awhile, like he was trying to figure out what had gone wrong in my upbringing. Then, finally, he'd ask me if I understood what he was trying to say.

"Yes," I'd answer. "You're trying to say I've embarrassed the family again."

That's when my father would shake his head and leave the room. On his way out, he'd mutter, "I might as well be talking to a brick wall."

I was still going over this pretend conversation in my mind when I heard the back door open. Within seconds, Dad's footsteps were pounding down the hall.

My heart began to race.

Knock, knock, knock.

"Who is it?" I asked nervously.

"You know who it is, Alex. It's Dad. I want to have a little talk with you."

I tried to stall.

"Who did you say it was again? Tad? I don't know any Tad."

"Dad!"

"Brad?"

He pounded. "Open the door, Alex! Now!"

"No, Dad. Please. I already know what you want. You want to talk to me about what happened today. Only it won't do any good. Talking isn't going to change anything. I blew it. I made a fool of myself and I ran out on my team. So if it's all the same to you, I'm just going to live right here in my room for the rest of my life. That way I won't ever bring shame on our family again. So if you could just shove a bologna sandwich under the door every day or so, I'd appreciate it."

I paused a minute.

"Well, okay. I guess that's it. It's been nice having you for a father, Father. I'm grateful for all you've tried to do for me. And I'm sorry I've been such a big disappointment."

I heaved a pathetic sigh.

On the other side of the door, there was nothing but silence. Finally, I heard the sound of Dad's footsteps as he walked away.

I was sure he was on his way to tell my mother how miserable I sounded. Then the two of them would put their heads together and try to think up a way to get me to come out of my room.

A few minutes later, he was back.

I felt warm all over. *Now that's a loving father,* I thought. *That's a father who isn't giving up on his kid.*

Pretty soon, I heard a rustling noise under my dresser. I got down on my stomach and looked.

It was a bologna sandwich in a plastic bag, being

squeezed underneath the little space at the bottom of my door!

I grabbed it and threw it in my trash can.

Parents! Just when you think you've got them figured out, they go and pull a lame stunt like that.

The next day was Sunday. Except for a few minutes while Mom and Dad were at church, I didn't come out of my room all day long.

It was awful being stuck in there. And what made it even worse was that my parents didn't seem bothered by it at all. They were going around the house laughing and talking like they didn't even *have* a son. Like they'd never even heard of me before.

The other thing I hated was how totally bored I was. Most of the time I just lay on my bed. There were a zillion things I could have done to amuse myself, but I couldn't risk it. If Mom decided to peek through my bedroom window to check on me, it couldn't look like I was having a good time.

By dinnertime, I wanted to come out of there so bad I couldn't stand it. I was starving. *Starving*, I tell you!

I had hardly eaten a thing all day. While my parents were at church, I had snuck a few snacks and a couple of apples, but it wasn't nearly enough to keep a growing boy alive. All I had left were two pretzels and one broken graham cracker. I tried putting the pretzels between the graham cracker pieces to make a sandwich, but it didn't look that appetizing.

Also, I hate to mention this, but starvation wasn't my only problem. I also needed to pay a little visit to the bathroom.

I did everything I could to put it off. I jumped up and down and crossed my legs and danced around till I couldn't stand it. But all of a sudden it was get-out-of-my-way-'cause-I'm-comin'-through! I shoved the dresser out of the way and streaked to the bathroom!

On the way back to my room, I heard Mom and Dad sitting down to eat. I could smell the delicious aroma of dinner all the way down the hall.

Mmmm. Was that fried chicken? And what else? Mashed potatoes, maybe?

My stomach growled loudly. How long can a person go without food before he passed out? I wondered. Maybe if I just got a little peek at it, I would feel better.

Quietly, I tiptoed down the hall. I stopped at the kitchen door and got down on my hands and knees. Then, slowly, I looked around the corner.

Yup! Just as I thought. Fried chicken! Mashed potatoes! And...ohmygosh! Was that corn on the cob?

My mouth watered so much that I drooled on the floor. Unfortunately, my parents chose that exact moment to look over.

I grinned sheepishly and wiped up the drool spot with my T-shirt.

They turned back around like they hadn't even noticed me.

"Oh, no, you don't! You can't look directly at a person and then pretend you don't see him. That's just dumb," I said.

My father shrugged. "You're the one who wanted to stay locked up for the rest of your life, Alex," he said. "You're the one who didn't want to be bothered. Mom and I are only trying to respect your wishes."

I stared at all that corn on the cob. "Yeah, well, there's been a change in my wishes," I said quietly. "My wishes now include a chicken dinner from time to time."

My father shrugged again. "Help yourself."

I hurried to the table and picked up my fork.

My mother glanced over at me. "Chicken," she said.

Geez! What was wrong with her, anyway? Couldn't she give it a rest?

"I'm not a chicken, Mother! I ran off the Little League field because I'd already blown it and I didn't know what else to do! But that doesn't mean I'm a chicken!"

Mom stared at me for quite a while. Finally, she turned to Dad and pointed at the food.

"Chicken?" she said.

After he had taken a piece, she turned back to me again. "Shall we try this one more time, Alex? Chicken?"

This time, I stuck my fork into a chicken breast and put it on my plate. I managed to mumble "thank you," but that was the last thing I said during the entire meal.

After I ate, I went back to my room and fed my graham-cracker-and-pretzel sandwich to my fish.

Then I took a shower and went straight to bed.

Tomorrow I would have to face the whole school. And something told me it was going to take every bit of strength I had.

chapter twelve

WHO WOULD HAVE THUNK IT?

One of the things I really hate about my mom is how she always knows when I'm lying. Don't ask me how she does it. I've tried to figure it out, but so far I've had no luck at all.

On Monday morning, when she came to get me out of bed, I moaned and groaned and held my sides. But she didn't buy it for a second. Instead, she just opened my blinds and smiled.

"What a nice sunny day it is out there," she said.

"Aggg...ooowww!" I cried out.

Mom rolled her eyes. "Okay, fine. I guess I'm supposed to play along and ask you what's wrong with your stomach."

I doubled over. "It's killing me, Mother. That's what's wrong. There must have been something wrong with my chicken last night."

Mom walked over to my fish bowl. "Did your fish have chicken for dinner, too?" she asked.

"Don't make jokes. This isn't funny," I told her.

"I'm not making a joke, Alex. Your fish is belly-up," she said.

I jumped out of bed and ran over to the bowl. "That's impossible. No! He can't be! I just bought him! He couldn't have croaked already!"

Mom looked closer. "Maybe he's faking it. Maybe he just wants us to flush him down the toilet so he can swim to the sea," she said.

I glared at her. "How can you make a joke about this? This is my dead pet we're talking about here."

"Oh, for heaven's sake, Alex. You go through at least one fish a week. You've only had that one for three days. How much can a three-day-old goldfish mean to you?"

"A lot, Mother. That's how much. For the past three days, that fish was the only friend I had."

I put my hand over my heart. "We shared our secrets and our dreams."

I thought a moment.

"Plus a graham cracker and two pretzels," I added quietly.

I got my fish net and scooped him up. Then I ran

97

him into the bathroom and flushed. I watched him swirl. Another buck-fifty right down the pot.

When I got back to my room, my mother was smiling.

"Well, I see that your stomach is better," she said. "You haven't moaned or groaned for several minutes."

I grabbed my sides and bent over.

"Forget it, Alex," she said. "You're going to school."

Geez! If it hadn't been for that stupid fish, I could have pulled it off! Man! You try to do your pet a favor by giving him a special snack and he pays you back by dying. How selfish and inconsiderate is *that?*

After breakfast, I walked to school as slowly as I could. I was trying to brace myself for all the teasing. There was going to be a ton of it, too. And what made it even worse was that T.J. Stoner was going to be leading the pack.

As I walked onto the playground, I saw T.J. standing at the water fountain. He didn't see me, though. That's because there were about a million little kids gathered around him, waving pieces of paper.

No. It can't be, I thought. *They're not asking him for his autograph, are they?*

I looked closer.

They were! All those dumb kids were actually asking T.J. to sign his name! Now he'd be more obnoxious than *ever*.

I hurried to my classroom. If only I could get to my desk before school started, maybe my teacher would keep everyone from making fun of me.

When I walked into the room, Mrs. Grayson was sitting at her desk. She looked at me and started to grin.

"Ooga ooga," she said.

I sucked in my cheeks.

"It wasn't 'ooga ooga,' Mrs. Grayson," I said, annoyed. "'Ooga ooga' is the sound an old-fashioned car makes. What I *said* was 'booga booga.'"

"Oh," she said, looking a little embarrassed. "Sorry. It was hard to hear you from the stands."

Okay. Now that she had that out of her system, maybe she'd help me out.

"Mrs. Grayson? I was wondering…would it be okay if I sat in the back of the room today?" I asked. "To tell you the truth, I'm not really sure what's going to happen when the rest of the kids get here. And I'm not really feeling that well."

Before she had a chance to answer, the bell rang and everyone started piling into class. T.J. Stoner was the first one through the door.

"Hey! Look who it is!" he hollered. "It's Booga Booga Frankovitch!"

Mrs. Grayson raised her eyebrows. "I see what you mean," she said to me. "Do you want to go to the nurse?"

I glared at T.J.

"No. Forget it," I said. "If I feel like I'm going to toss my cookies, I'll just aim for T.J. He's a pretty good catch."

T.J. pretended to shiver. "Ooooo…what a threat," he said. "If you toss your cookies like you toss a baseball, you'll miss me by a mile."

"Okay. That's enough, boys," said Mrs. Grayson. "Sit. Both of you."

I was glad she stepped in. For the first time in my life, I didn't have a comeback.

As soon as he was in his seat, T.J. raised his hand. "Mrs. Grayson, I've been signing autographs outside, and there are a couple I didn't get to yet. Would you mind if I finished signing while you're taking attendance?"

Mrs. Grayson practically burst with pride. "Why, certainly not, T.J. I think I can allow the Little League Pitching Champion to sign a few autographs."

Then she stood up at her desk.

"Boys and girls," she said loudly. "In case any of

100

you missed it on the news, our very own T.J. Stoner has been entered into the Little League record books. He even made the national news, didn't you, T.J.?"

He nodded proudly. "ESPN," he said.

Mrs. Grayson continued. "T.J. Stoner now holds the official record for the most games ever won in a row in the history of Little League baseball. And it's really been exciting to have him in our class this year."

She started to clap. Then everyone else clapped, too.

Everyone except me, that is. I was busy scribbling a message to Brian. It read:

Say something nice about me and I'll give you five bucks after school.

Brian's hand shot in the air like a bullet.

"Yes, Brian?" said Mrs. Grayson.

"Mrs. Grayson, I think we're also fortunate to have Alex Frankovitch in our class this year. If you ask me, it took a tremendous amount of courage to stand in front of a crowd full of strangers and make a complete idiot of himself, like Alex did on Saturday."

Everybody cracked up. Even Mrs. Grayson couldn't keep from laughing.

If I ever become famous, Brian Dunlop will be the first friend I'll dump.

The rest of the day I tried to stay as quiet as I could I wanted to make it as easy as possible for people to ignore me. But it didn't do any good. All day long, kids kept walking past my desk, whispering "booga booga" in my ear. Then they'd walk away laughing, like they were the first person in the history of the universe to have thought of such a clever thing.

By the middle of the afternoon I'd totally had it with the booga booga jokes. That's when Harold Marshall raised his hand and asked if he could sharpen his pencil. Harold's a troublemaker, so right away I was suspicious.

I watched him get out of his seat and turn down my aisle. I was positive he was going to try something. Only *this* time, things were going to be different.

As Harold got closer to my seat, I got ready for him.

Here he comes...here he comes...okay...okay... NOW!

Just as Harold started to lean over and whisper, I quickly turned my cheek and leaned in his direction.

Then I jumped up and hollered. "SICK! SICK!" I yelled, wiping off my face. "HAROLD MARSHALL JUST KISSED ME! HOW DISGUSTING!"

Harold turned bright red. "I did not! I did not kiss you!" he sputtered.

I pointed at my face. "Then how did my cheek get so wet? Huh, Harold?" I asked. "Mrs. Grayson, can I go to the bathroom and wash it off? It's totally slimy and slobbery."

Mrs. Grayson waved me out the door and ordered Harold to sit down. As I left the room, I saw several kids covering their faces as Harold passed by. It was the high point of my day.

Unfortunately, though, making fun of Harold didn't really put an end to my problem. As soon as I got back from the bathroom, the booga boogas started all over again.

I looked at the clock. Forty-five minutes to go. I didn't know if I could make it that long. I was really feeling down. Nothing I ever did turned out right. *Nothing.* Even when I did something well, like bunting, it turned out wrong.

Face it, Alex. The only thing you're good at is being a runt. You're nothing. A big, fat nothing!

I put my head down and rested it on my desk. I felt my eyes start filling up with tears.

Great. This is perfect. Now big, fat nothing Alex Frankovitch is going to cry in front of the whole class. A perfect ending to a perfect day.

Suddenly, I heard my name being called. "Alex

103

Frankovitch?" said the voice. "Is Alex Frankovitch there?"

Quickly, I wiped my face and looked up. The voice was coming from the loudspeaker on the wall. Oh, geez! It was our principal, Mr. Vernon!

"Mrs. Grayson? Can you hear me? Is Alex Frankovitch in class right now?" he asked.

"Yes he is, Mr. Vernon," she answered. "Would you like me to send him down to your office?"

"No," said Mr. Vernon. "I have an announcement to make and I just wanted to be sure that he was there."

T.J. looked at me and laughed. We both knew what was coming. Mr. Vernon was going to take this opportunity to make a couple of booga booga jokes so the whole school could have a good laugh before the bell.

He clicked on the speakers to the other classrooms.

"Attention, boys and girls, may I have your attention, please? First of all, would like to congratulate T.J. Stoner on his brilliant Little League performance. The entire school is extremely proud of his achievement, and I think that we should all give him a big round of applause."

He stopped talking so that every kid in the whole school could applaud. You could hear it echoing up and down the halls.

"I have already spoken to T.J. today," Mr. Vernon continued, "and he has agreed to stay after school in case any of you would like to stop by and get his autograph. We'll have a table set up for him in the Media Center."

T.J. put his arms behind his head and leaned his chair back on two legs like a big shot. One little slip would have sent him sprawling…but no such luck.

Mr. Vernon's voice came back on. "Okay…now for the surprise. There's someone else in Mrs. Grayson's sixth-grade room who also deserves congratulations. It seems that Alex Frankovitch has also made quite a name for himself."

I swallowed hard. *Here it comes*, I thought. Tears started to fill my eyes again, but I forced them back into my head.

"I have just received news from his mother that today, Alex Frankovitch received a letter in the mail announcing that he is the winner of the national Kitty Fritters Television Contest."

What? What did he just say?

"As his prize, Alex will get to appear in a national television commercial!" continued Mr. Vernon. "Congratulations, Alex! We're all very excited about having one of our students become a big TV star!"

For a second, the whole class was stunned. No one could believe what Mr. Vernon had said. Especially *me!* I only wrote that letter as a joke! I

105

was making fun of Kitty Fritters! How could I have won?

At last, Mrs. Grayson stood up and started to clap. Then the rest of the class clapped with her. She told me to take a bow, but my legs were so weak I couldn't get out of my chair. So I just waved and let it go at that.

Suddenly, I saw my mother standing in the door-way. Mrs. Grayson went to greet her. They called me into the hall.

Mom hugged me and tousled my hair. "How was *that* for a great surprise? I was coming to tell you in person, but I happened to see Mr. Vernon on the way down the hall, and we decided it would be more fun to do it this way. Were you surprised?"

I nodded. It's hard to form words when your mouth is hanging wide open in shock.

"When do you get to do the commercial?" asked Mrs. Grayson.

"I…I…I'm not sure," I managed, at last. "I mean I don't even remember what the prize was. I just entered that contest for laughs."

My mother waved a piece of paper in front of my face. "Well, it's no joke anymore," she said. "It says here that the commercial will be made in New York City, sometime within the next six months. They also said that your essay was the craziest, most original entry they had ever received, and they can't wait to meet you!"

Mrs. Grayson shook my hand. "There. Now I bet someday I'll be able to say I shook hands with a major movie star."

She and my mother both laughed. But the more I thought about it, the more I thought she might be right. After all, I *am* an original. And I'm certainly *crazy*. I smiled at the thought of it. What more could Hollywood want?

After a few minutes, my mother went home and Mrs. Grayson and I went back in the room. Since it was almost time for the bell, she told us to put our work away. Then she called T.J. to the front of the room with me.

"Since this is such a special day for our class, why don't we spend the rest of it interviewing our two class celebrities like they do on TV?"

Reluctantly, T.J. sat down on the edge of her desk next to me. It was pretty clear that a lot of the joy had gone out of his day. He really hated sharing the spotlight.

"Okay," said Mrs. Grayson. "Who wants to ask the first question?"

Harold Marshall jumped right up.

"I have a question for Alex," he said, still hoping to get back at me. "What exactly is a booga booga?"

Thoughtfully, I rubbed my chin. "Hmm…well, Harold, it's a little hard to explain," I said. "A booga booga is sort of this gooky, yellowish, slimy…wait a minute! What a stroke of luck. If everyone will turn around quickly, I believe there's a booga booga stuck on Harold's front tooth!"

Harold turned red again. He closed his mouth and sat down. Some kids never learn.

After that, nobody gave me any more trouble. T.J. and I started answering questions. Melissa Phillips asked each of us who our most famous relative was.

T.J. said it was his brother, Matt Stoner.

I said it was my grandmother, Tino Martinez.

Most of the questions were aimed at T.J. But I didn't mind it at all. It felt good just sitting up there, you know? Just sitting in the front of the room like some big shot celebrity.

Every once in a while, I glanced over at T.J. as he was talking. The kid was a jerk, all right. But for the first time, I began to think that maybe it wasn't entirely his fault. I had a feeling that being treated like a big shot celebrity can turn almost any kid into a jerk if they're not careful. Even a wonderful person such as myself.

Pretty soon the bell rang. I went to my desk and picked up my homework books. As I passed by Mrs. Grayson, she winked.

I winked back. What do you know? After all these years I think it's finally happened. I think I've finally found a teacher who appreciates my sense of humor.

Outside the building, Brian was waiting for me. He and I still had a score to settle.

"Oh, no, you don't, Brian," I said. "Just because I've suddenly become famous and popular, it doesn't mean you can come crawling back to me. I'm not forgetting what you said back there today"

Brian looked puzzled. "Who's crawling back? I'm waiting to collect the five bucks you owe me for saying something nice."

"Idiot? Idiot is *nice?*"

Brian threw his hands in the air. "Man, that's just like you, Alex!" he complained. "Already you've forgotten the compliment! I mean if I had only called you an idiot, I would understand why you were upset. But I called you a *complete* idiot. A one hundred percent idiot. Come on, Alex. Where's the appreciation here?"

I couldn't help but smile. The thing is, I *am* a complete idiot. So how could I stay mad at my best friend?

We started walking home together. A couple of kids came up and congratulated me on the TV commercial. No one asked for an autograph, but that will probably come later.

109

On the way home, Brian and I talked a lot about my future as a comedian. We decided that as long as I've already gotten my first break into show business, I might as well go on to become disgustingly rich and famous. Brian said we could be a team. He volunteered to help me write my material. *Material* is the word comedians use when they talk about their jokes.

Even now, I can't believe it. Me, skinny little Alex Frankovitch...a *star*.

I wonder if the Kitty Fritters people will want me to read my winning essay on the commercial. Probably not. The part about how they taste like rubber wouldn't be good for business.

They'll probably just want to use a close-up of my adorable little face.

I just hope they don't want me to do anything dumb. Like one time I saw a cereal commercial where they made this little kid dress up like a raisin and dance around a big bowl of oatmeal. They wouldn't make me do something stupid like that, would they?

Hmmm. Maybe it's time for another little talk with you-know-who...

"Hello, God? It's Alex again. Listen...as you've probably heard, I'm going to be on a TV commercial soon. And I would *really* appreciate it if you'd keep an eye out for me. I mean, I don't mind making a fool of myself once in a while, God, but if it's all the same to you, I'd rather not dress up like a Kitty Fritter and dance around a cat dish. I do have my limits, you know.

"Are you there, God? Are you paying attention? If you would just do me this one little favor, I promise to stop singing 'Ahchoo' at the end of the hymns in church and start singing 'Amen' like everyone else. How's that? Is it a deal, God? If it is, maybe you could show me by making the wind start blowing.

"I'm waiting…I'm waiting here, God…

"Hey! I saw it! That little leaf on that tree over there. It blew in the wind! I'm sure of it! Thank you! Thank you, God! I *knew* I could count on you!

"And remember, if you ever need a favor, you can count on me, too.

"Just look me up in New York or Hollywood.

"I'll be in the Yellow Pages…

"Under STAR."

BARBARA PARK is one of today's funniest, most popular writers for middle graders. Her novels, which include *Skinnybones, The Kid in the Red Jacket, Mick Harte was Here, Maxie, Rosie, and Earl—Partners in Grime,* and *Rosie Swanson: Fourth-Grade Geek for President,* have won just about every award given by children.

She has also created the Junie B. Jones character for Random House. Recent books about Junie include *Junie B. Jones and Some Sneaky Peeky Spying* and *Junie B. Jones and Her Big Fat Mouth.*

Ms. Park earned a B.S. degree in education at the University of Alabama and lives in Paradise Valley, Arizona, with her husband.

It was his big break...or was it?

ALMOST STARRING SKINNYBONES

by Barbara Park

When Alex Frankovitch—better known as Skinnybones—gets the chance to star in a TV commercial, it seems as though his dreams have come true. Who cares if it's just a cat food commercial and he plays a six-year-old wearing a dorky coonskin cap? It's still national television—and a rare opportunity to thumb his nose at his classmates. So why does the Alex Frankovitch Fan Club attract only two members—a cat and a toddler? And why do all the kids laugh hysterically every time they see him? Is this the end of Skinnybones' career as a Big Celebrity?

"Park is laugh-out-loud funny!" —*Booklist*

"Once again demonstrating her remarkable ear for dialogue, Park also shows a good sense of timing in this fast-paced outing."

—*School Library Journal*

PUBLISHED BY RANDOM HOUSE, INC.

THE KID IN THE RED JACKET

It was bad enough that Howard's parents moved the family to a street called Chester Pewe, but now they want him to be nice to his tag-along neighbor, who happens to be a six-year-old girl. How do they expect him to make any *real* friends with her around? At this rate, he could spend the rest of his life known only by the color of his sportswear!

Winner of a **Parents' Choice** *Gold Award*
An **IRA-CBC** *Children's Choice*

PUBLISHED BY RANDOM HOUSE, INC.

Politics Isn't Pretty...

ROSIE SWANSON: FOURTH-GRADE GEEK FOR PRESIDENT

Rosie Swanson has always considered it her duty to make sure that the authorities are aware of what's going on in her school. So what if her classmates think she's a geek and a snitch? *She* knows that she's only doing her job. Now, to help fight for the good of the school, she's decided to run for president of the fourth grade. But how does someone like Rosie defeat popular kids like Alan Allen and Summer Lynne Jones? With the help of her pals Maxie and Earl, Rosie comes up with a brilliant campaign. She even fights her urge to tattle, and forces herself to "be nice to people who make you puke." But when Alan starts stealing Rosie's campaign slogans, it's time to watch out! You just don't mess with Nosy Rosie...

"Right on target...a very good read."　　　*—Booklist*

"As bright and funny as they come."

—Kirkus Reviews

PUBLISHED BY RANDOM HOUSE, INC.

OPERATION: DUMP THE CHUMP

Ever since his little brother, Robert (not so affection-
ately known as the Slobert), showed up, he's special-
ized in ruining Oscar's life. He even took Oscar's under-
wear to school for show-and-tell! Oscar decides he's
had enough and comes up with a wickedly brilliant,
top-secret scheme to get the ultimate revenge. It'll take
stealth, courage, and determination. But if he can carry
off Operation: Dump the Chump without a hitch, he'll
have a present better than money can buy—a Slobert-
free summer!

Winner of Indiana's Young Hoosier Award
Winner of the Tennessee Children's Choice Award

MY MOTHER GOT MARRIED (AND OTHER DIASASTERS)

What about me?

Charlie Hickle's life has become a three-ring circus. Why did his mom have to get remarried anyway? Now there are way too many people in one house. First there's his new stepfather, the nature guy. Then there's his five-year-old stepbrother, Thomas the Pest, who's Charlie's new roommate. Worst of all, Charlie has to deal with his stepsister, Lydia the phone-hog. His mom assures him that things will work out eventually. But Charlie isn't interested in *eventually*. He wants things back the way they used to be—*right now*!

PUBLISHED BY RANDOM HOUSE, INC.

DEAR ESIE, HELP ME! LOVE, EARL

MAXIE, ROSIE, AND EARL— PARTNERS IN GRIME

The three biggest dweebs in school...

Meet Maxie, Rosie, and Earl—three kids who meet as they await their doom at the principal's office. Shy Earl is there because he refused to read out loud in class. Nosy Rosie is in trouble because her teacher is sick of her tattling. And then there's Maxie, who finally got tired of being teased and took matters into his own hands. Now they wait like three sitting ducks. But no matter what the outcome may be, these three bumbling outlaws have just begun the start of a memorable relationship...

"Park does it again. Here's a book so funny, readers can't help but laugh out loud." —*Booklist*

PUBLISHED BY RANDOM HOUSE, INC.

DEAR GOD, HELP!!! LOVE, EARL

Looking for a nice, warm hiding spot...

Wimpy Earl Wilber has just met death, and his name is Eddie McFee. Eddie is the meanest, toughest kid in the fifth grade, and Earl has to pay him one dollar a week to keep Eddie from beating him up. Luckily, Earl's pals, Rosie the Snoop and Maxie the Brain, have decided to help him out. Maxie has a brilliant plan that should keep Eddie out of Earl's life for good. Now all Earl has to do is pretend to be dead...

PUBLISHED BY RANDOM HOUSE, INC.